'I wouldn't ha
girl for one-nig

'But then, in spite of all your research, you still don't know a great deal about me,' Zanna parried.

Jake's mouth quirked. 'I'd have said we were intimately acquainted,' he drawled.

'You're quite right, of course. I don't usually behave as I did that night, and I don't want to be reminded of it—or to repeat it either.'

'That was not what I was suggesting... Have dinner with me tonight.'

It was more a command than a request. 'I'm busy...'

He tutted. 'Playing hard to get?'

'Not before time, perhaps,' she said with cool irony. 'I'm sure you've heard the saying about ships that pass in the night. I'd like to leave it like that.'

He shook his head. The dark eyes held hers almost mesmerically. 'We didn't pass... We collided.'

Dear Reader,

Is it really twenty-one years since I sent in that first script, so unversed in the ways of publishing that I forgot to include any return postage?

In the event it wasn't needed. *Garden of Dreams* emerged from the pile, somehow, and was published.

I'd done it. I'd achieved the ambition I'd cherished since I was five years old. I was a real novelist.

I sat back to bask in my own glory, but not for long. A crisp editorial request for book number two 'as soon as possible, please' soon wiped away the smug smile.

Did they mean it? Was I really expected to ride that emotional rollercoaster all over again with another heroine? Surely not.

Now, fifty rides on, I still get the same thrill as I plunge into the unknown with a new cast of characters.

I hope you share my pleasure. Thank you for keeping me company.

Sara Craven

Sara Craven was born in South Devon and grew up surrounded by books in a house by the sea. After leaving grammar school she worked as a local journalist, covering everything from flower shows to murders. She started writing for Mills & Boon in 1975. Apart from writing, her passions include films, music, cooking and eating in good restaurants. She now lives in Somerset.

Recent titles by the same author:

ULTIMATE TEMPTATION

ONE RECKLESS NIGHT

BY
SARA CRAVEN

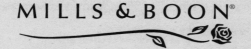

MILLS & BOON®

All the characters in this book have no existence outside the imagination of the author, and have no relation whatsoever to anyone bearing the same name or names. They are not even distantly inspired by any individual known or unknown to the author, and all the incidents are pure invention.

First published in Great Britain 1997
Harlequin Mills & Boon Limited,
Eton House, 18-24 Paradise Road, Richmond, Surrey TW9 1SR

© Sara Craven 1997

ISBN 0 263 80355 4

Set in Times Roman 10½ on 11½ pt.
01-9709-55059 C1

Printed and bound in Great Britain
by Mackays of Chatham PLC, Chatham

CHAPTER ONE

ZANNA WESTCOTT walked into the sitting room of her hotel suite and shut the door behind her. For a moment she stood still, confronting the trim image reflected back from the mirror on the wall opposite from the sleek blonde hair, swept severely back from her forehead, and the uncluttered lines of the black business suit and crisp white shirt down to the slender dark-stockinged legs and small feet in low-heeled pumps. All cool, tailored control.

She took a deep breath, then, shattering the image, lifted an arm, punching the air in sheer exultation as her face splintered into a monkey grin of triumph.

'I did it,' she told herself aloud, her green eyes dancing. 'I actually did it.'

She hadn't been able to show her feelings in the hotel conference room just now as the deal had finally been agreed. The atmosphere had been too heavy, too laden with disappointment as yet another family-owned company went under the hammer.

Yet what had they really expected? She'd laid down the terms the previous afternoon, coolly and briskly, making it clear there was no room for manoeuvre, unfazed when the offer was rejected out of hand.

If they'd thought a twenty-five-year-old woman was a soft touch, they now knew differently, she thought.

She had smiled politely, outlined the probable alternatives, advised them to reconsider overnight and added with emphasis that she would require their final answer at ten o'clock the following morning.

As soon as she'd walked into the conference room the unhappy, resigned faces had told her all she'd wanted to know.

Reason had prevailed and Westcott Holdings had acquired another useful piece of property. Notched up another victory.

My victory, she thought. Alone and unaided.

Still smiling, she walked across to the phone and dialled her father's private direct line at Westcott Holdings.

'Sir Gerald Westcott's office. How may I help you?'

Zanna's lips tightened in disappointment as she heard the clipped tones of Tessa Lloyd, her father's personal assistant. She said, 'I'd like to speak to him, please, Tessa.'

'I'm sorry, Miss Westcott. Sir Gerald is in a meeting. He asked me to take any message.'

Zanna was tempted to shout childishly, I don't want to leave a message! She wanted to speak to her father in person, to tell him about her achievement. Maybe this time to hear his voice soften with love and pride as he said, Well done.

She should have known there'd be a meeting, but all the same she'd hoped he'd be available. More fool me, she thought, feeling oddly—even absurdly—deflated.

Instead she said coolly, 'I see. Then please tell him he now owns Zolto Electronics at a much lower price than we originally hoped.'

'That's excellent news, Miss Westcott.' There was no great expression in the even tone. 'I'm sure Sir Gerald will be delighted. I presume you'll be returning immediately?'

That had been her intention, but there was something in the other woman's tone, an assumption that she could simply be called to heel, which ignited an unwonted spark of rebellion in Zanna.

She said, to her own surprise, 'Actually, no. I'm taking the rest of the day off. And the weekend,' she added recklessly. 'I'll be back in the office on Monday.'

'But, Miss Westcott.' Tessa Lloyd sounded shocked. 'I'm sure Sir Gerald will be waiting for a full report as soon as possible.'

'I was told to leave a message,' Zanna returned. 'That's the message I'm leaving. Goodbye, Tessa.'

She put the phone down firmly before any more protests could be formulated. Her father might think highly of Tessa Lloyd's efficiency but she wasn't particularly likeable, Zanna thought broodingly. And she guarded her employer like some jealous mother hen.

And now you've let her needle you into a forty-eight-hour break that you don't need and don't know what to do with anyway, she chided herself crossly.

She glanced round at her suite, restlessly absorbing the opulently bland furnishings, the forgettable series of prints which adorned the walls, the overly tasteful arrangement of silk flowers on a gilt table against a wall.

Suddenly she felt stifled—almost claustrophobic.

Instead of telephoning she would go down to Reception and tell them she was staying on. This was a city, after all. It had a theatre, restaurants. She would plan herself an evening's entertainment, make the appropriate reservations. There would be art galleries and museums she could visit during the rest of her stay. It would be fun. Or at least different, she amended, with a wry twist of the lips.

The foyer was busy when she emerged from the lift, and the receptionists standing in line at the long desk were all fully occupied. Zanna picked up one of the complimentary folders intended for tourists, detailing things to see and do in the area, and began to leaf idly through it.

A voice at her shoulder said quietly, 'Miss Westcott.'

Turning with a start, she saw Henry Walton, the chairman of Zolto Electronics, his lined face tired and defeated.

He said, 'I wanted to congratulate you, Miss Westcott. You have a bargain—as, of course, you know.'

'Yes.' Zanna lifted her chin, her expression challenging. 'I hope there are no hard feelings.'

He shook his head with a faint smile. 'No, that is too much to ask.' He studied her for a moment, his eyes suddenly sharp and shrewd, giving her a glimpse of the man who had built up a company from a dream only to see it ultimately undermined by the recession.

He said, with a sigh, 'Yes, you're your father's own daughter, Miss Westcott. And please don't think I mean that as a compliment. Instead, I'm almost sorry for you.' He inclined his head with a kind of remote courtesy and walked away.

Zanna stared after him, as shocked and winded as if he'd actually raised his fist and struck her.

It had been the quietest of exchanges yet she suddenly felt self-conscious, as if everyone in the hotel lobby had turned to look at her. As if she were suddenly naked under their censorious gaze.

Her sense of achievement, her plans for the evening ahead suddenly went by the board. She felt chilled and oddly uncertain.

'May I help you?' One of the receptionists was free, her brows raised enquiringly, her smile plastic and professional.

Zanna shook her head, then turned away, the edge of the folder still biting into her hand. Her immediate intention was to go back to her room. Instead, she found herself headed, almost running, for the main exit to the hotel car park.

With the thought, I've got to get out of here—I must...beating in her head like a drum.

The motorway service station was like any other. Zanna selected a plate of mixed salad and a pot of coffee and carried them to an empty table.

What an idiot, she thought with vexation, to have allowed that little encounter to push her off-balance like that. Normally she wouldn't have leapt into the car and driven off without the slightest idea where she was heading.

And why was she so disturbed anyway? Being Gerald Westcott's daughter—being recognised as such—was something to be proud of. Whereas there was nothing admirable in admitting defeat—in failing. That was a lesson she'd been taught since her earliest years.

Achievement—coming first—was the name of the game. Getting the best results at school. Knowing that less would only provoke some disapproving comment from the man she wanted so desperately to please. Any kind of second-best was unthinkable. Times were hard. You had to be tough. There was no room for sentiment in business.

This was the armour she dressed in each morning. The armour in which Henry Walton had found an unexpected and unwelcome chink.

How dared he feel sorry for her? she thought rawly. She didn't need anyone's pity. She had a flat overlooking the Thames, an expense account, a new car every year—and she'd just scored her first major negotiating success. She had everything going for her.

She gave a mental shrug as she sat down. Mr Walton had simply turned out to be a bad loser, which, although

something of a surprise, was his problem, and she was
a fool to let his remarks get to her. Although they'd
certainly taken the edge off her triumph, she thought
restively. Soured the day when she had totally justified
her place on her father's top team.

She was half tempted to change her mind and return
to London, except it might be seen as a kind of climb-
down, and the thought of Tessa Lloyd's superior smile
as she obeyed the tug on the leash cemented her determination to stay away, however briefly.

She still had the hotel's information folder on the table
beside her. She'd stop this aimless pounding up the
motorway and find something positive to do for the rest
of the day.

As she picked up the folder a pale green leaflet flut-
tered to the floor. Something about a series of spring art
exhibitions in local village halls. Nothing she would normally have noticed. But as she bent to retrieve the paper
the name 'Emplesham' seemed to leap out at her.

For a moment she was very still, staring down at it.
Remembering.

Emplesham, she thought wonderingly. It hadn't even
occurred to her how close it must be.

Yet once she'd have known. And without any prompt-
ing either. When she was a child, she'd looked it up
almost obsessively on the map, calculating the distance
from London, from boarding school—from anywhere,
she remembered, wincing—and promising herself that
one day she'd go there. See the place where the mother
she'd never known had been born. As if that, somehow,
would bring her closer.

And now I'm actually in the neighbourhood, and if I
hadn't seen this leaflet I wouldn't have given it a second
thought, she told herself wryly.

It was evidence, she realised, of how far she'd grown away from that lonely, introspective little girl.

And perhaps that was how it should stay. After all, going to look at the outside of a house wouldn't answer any of the questions which had bewildered and tormented her for so many years. The questions that her father, too racked by the grief of his loss, had always refused even to discuss.

After Susan Westcott's death he had sold the house they had shared, and its contents, dismissed the domestic staff and moved to a new locality with his baby daughter, Suzannah. From then on, of course, she had been always known as Zanna, as if even the similarities in their names were too painful for him to contemplate.

There were no mementoes, no photographs anywhere, and no one the child could ask about her mother. The only reminder that Sir Gerald seemed able to tolerate was the strangely disturbing portrait of his wife kept in his study.

It had always worried Zanna. Nor was it really a likeness either. Above the vibrant swirl of her crimson blouse Sue Westcott's face was a pale blur, the features barely suggested, apart from her eyes which seemed to burn with a wild green flame. Desperate eyes, Zanna had decided as she grew up. She'd found herself wondering whether her mother had known, somehow, how little time she had left to live. As a picture, it revealed little more.

And then on her eleventh birthday she'd received a small packet at her boarding school, the accompanying lawyer's letter stating that her mother's former nanny, Miss Grace Moss, had directed in her will that Zanna should be sent the enclosed.

It had been a small leather-bound photo album, full of ageing snapshots of people she didn't know in clothes from bygone years, and for a moment Zanna had been bewildered as to why this stranger should have bothered.

Then she'd seen that the last few photographs were all marked 'Church House, Emplesham' on the back. The first one was dated—'1950, Susan two days old'—and showed a woman in a neat dress and apron, presumably Nanny Moss, smiling in the wisteria-hung doorway of a long white house, with a tiny baby held protectively in her arms.

Others showed a small blonde girl playing among tall hollyhocks and delphiniums in a garden, or riding a tricycle, until finally a taller Sue had proudly showed off a new school hat and blazer.

Zanna had thought, *Mummy*, and her eyes had filled with tears. But she'd been grateful that she at last had something tangible to hold on to.

From that moment on the album went everywhere with her and became her most cherished possession, almost a talisman. But at the same time the way the bequest had been made had warned her, young though she was, that her father might not regard it in quite the same light, and that this was a gift to be kept secret, not shared with him.

She didn't want him to be unhappy again, and the only times she had ever pressed him for information about her mother he had become so angry and upset that she'd been almost frightened. His unresolved pain and grief for his late wife was his one weakness. The only sign of vulnerability he'd ever shown.

All these years she'd kept the secret, she thought ruefully, and the album occupied an inside pocket in her bag even now. Her sole and private link with the past.

Zanna took it out and flicked through it while she ate her meal.

It was probably a wild-goose chase, but there might

be someone in the village who'd remember the little girl
at Church House, who could help wipe out the apparent
vacuum that Sue Westcott had left in her wake.

At any rate, she would have to go and see.

After all, she argued, what do I have to lose?

Almost within minutes of taking the appropriate
motorway exit she found herself in a maze of country
lanes. The day was warm for late spring, and Zanna
opened the sun roof and slung her jacket into the back
of the car.

It wasn't a fast journey. Every bend in the road
seemed to reveal some new hazard—a tractor idling
along, a group of riders on horseback, a pair of motorists
who'd stopped to exchange the time of day, thereby
blocking the lane completely.

Even the throb of the motorway traffic was extin-
guished by birdsong and the bleating of sheep. Zanna
had the crazy sensation that she'd stepped backwards
into some time-warp, where life moved at a different,
slower pace.

Usually she would have been impatient, pushing herself and others, looking for a way round the obstacles in
her path. But today she felt herself slowing in unison.
She was aware that the tension was seeping out of her,
that the sun and the warm breeze with its scent of hedge-
rows were bestowing a kind of benison.

Someone had once said that to travel hopefully was
better than to arrive. For the first time she could understand that, and agree.

The Emplesham village sign was emblazoned on a
huge circle of stone half-buried in long grass and haw-
thorn at the side of the road.

As Zanna passed it she began to realise that all was
not well with her car. The engine note was not right. It
seemed to have developed a kind of stutter, she thought

with dismay. And then, without further warning, it died on her altogether.

Using the slight downward slope, Zanna steered the car onto the verge and applied the handbrake. She said under her breath, 'I don't believe this.' It was as if the damned thing had become suddenly bewitched as it crossed the village line. Although that, of course, was nonsense.

She could see roofs and the church tower only a couple of hundred yards away. There'd be help there, or at least a telephone, she decided. She locked the car and began to walk down the lane, only to see ahead of her, as she rounded the first corner, a small garage and workshop.

Thank goodness for that, at least, she thought as she picked her way between the limited selection of second-hand cars on the forecourt and entered the workshop.

She could hear music playing—one of Bach's Brandenburg Concertos, she recognised with slight incredulity—but could see no one. She moved forward uncertainly and nearly stumbled over a pair of long denim-clad legs protruding from under a car. And not just any car, she realised. It was a classic Jaguar—by no means new, but immaculately maintained.

A portable cassette player near the legs was presumably the source of the music.

Zanna raised her voice above it. 'Could you help me, please?'

There was no response, so she bent down and switched off the cassette.

She said, on a crisper note, 'Excuse me.'

There was a brief pause, then the owner of the legs disentangled himself from beneath the car and sat up, looking at her.

He was tall and lean, his mane of black curling hair

shaggy and unkempt. From a tanned face dark eyes surveyed her expressionlessly. His T-shirt and jeans were filthy with oil. He looked, Zanna thought with faint contempt, like some kind of gipsy.

Still, any port in a storm, she consoled herself, with a faint sigh. And if someone was actually allowing him to work on a car like that, he couldn't be totally incompetent.

He said, 'Consider yourself excused.' His voice was low-pitched, with a faint drawl and a barely detectable undercurrent of amusement.

Zanna stiffened slightly, needled by his continuing and lingering scrutiny. He would, she thought, know her again. She looked back at him coldly, registering in her turn a beak of a nose that had clearly been broken at some time, a cool, thin-lipped mouth and a chin with a determined tilt. An image not as easily dismissed as she'd first assumed.

She said briefly, 'My car has broken down.'

He shrugged. Through a rip in his shirt his shoulder looked very brown. 'It happens,' he returned laconically. 'My commiserations.' And he moved as if to slide back under the Jaguar.

'Just a moment,' Zanna said with a snap, and he paused enquiringly. She took a breath. 'I'm not looking for sympathy. I'd actually like you to fix it—if it's not too much trouble,' she added witheringly.

'Now that's the problem.' His face was solemn, but under their heavy lids she could swear his eyes were dancing. 'I am rather busy already. As you can see.'

'Yes, but I have an emergency,' Zanna said impatiently. 'And this is a garage.'

'Ten out of ten for observation.'

'And you operate a call-out service,' she went on. 'It says so on the board outside.'

He wiped his hands on a piece of rag. 'I'll say this for you—you're persistent,' he remarked flatly. He slowly uncoiled himself and stood up. It seemed to take for ever. Zanna had always considered herself a reasonable height, but he towered head and shoulders above her.

Oddly intimidated, she found herself taking an involuntary step backwards. Her heel slipped in a patch of oil and she stumbled.

'Careful.' His hand shot out and gripped her arm to steady her.

'I'm all right,' she snapped, shrugging herself free and receiving a frankly sardonic look in return.

'Well, you could have fooled me,' he drawled. 'Are you always this nervous?'

No, of course she wasn't, and her overreaction to what had only been, after all, a fleeting contact vexed her.

She shrugged. 'I'm just—anxious about my car.'

He sighed. 'What seems to be the problem with it?' he asked, without enthusiasm.

'The engine made a stuttering noise and just—stopped,' she said rather lamely.

The firm mouth quirked. 'Did it, now? Well, I suggest you go back to the poor thing and take a good hard look at the petrol gauge.'

Zanna gasped. 'I filled the tank before I left the motorway,' she said stonily. 'And I can do without the patronising remarks.'

His face hardened. 'Just as I can do without the aggravation. Try one of the motoring organisations, lady. They're obliged to be pleasant.'

Zanna bit her lip. 'But that could take hours,' she objected. 'Whereas you'd only have to walk up the road.' She drew another breath. 'Look, whatever the going rate is, I'll pay you double.'

'There speaks the complete autocrat.' There was no doubting the amusement in his voice now, or the accompanying touch of contempt. 'I have news for you, sweetheart. Market economy notwithstanding, not everyone's for sale.'

'With an attitude like yours, I'm surprised you have a business at all,' Zanna retorted hotly. 'Or do they take whatever they can get in this backwater?'

'Pretty much,' he said. 'Although I understand they've stopped flogging the peasants and selling their children into slavery.' The dark eyes swept her from head to foot again. 'However, if it's such a dump, why are you honouring it with your presence.'

'I'm not,' she denied curtly. 'I'm just passing through.'

'An interesting trick,' he said. 'Especially as the road comes to a dead end at Hollins Farm. Maybe you should trade the car in for a juggernaut, if you plan to drive over it. Or even an amphibious vehicle,' he added reflectively. 'Ted Hollins has a duck pond.'

For the first time in years she was tempted to the schoolgirl rudeness of sticking her tongue out at him, but managed to restrain herself. She simply could not afford to alienate him further.

Smile as if genuinely amused, she ordered herself through gritted teeth. 'Actually,' she said, with studied brightness, 'I've come to see the art exhibition.'

His brows lifted. 'It's a very local affair. No Picassos or Van Goghs. You won't need your American Express.' He paused meditatively before adding, 'But I guess it'll keep you occupied while I'm looking at your car.'

'Thank you.' Her voice was glacial and his grin widened.

'Keys?'

Reluctantly Zanna dropped them into his outstretched hand.

He nodded and walked past her into the sunlight with an easy, long-legged stride. 'I'll see you later.'

Needled by his casual dismissal, she hurried after him. 'Where, exactly?'

He swung round and looked at her. The dark eyes seemed to burn suddenly into hers. He said softly, 'Oh, I'll find you.'

It could have been a threat. It might have been a promise.

But for one startling, inexplicable moment, the breath caught in her throat and her pulses juddered in a strange mixture of excitement and something bordering on panic. She nodded abruptly, then turned away and began to walk towards the village.

And she knew, before she'd gone fifty yards, that if she glanced back over her shoulder she would find him watching her.

CHAPTER TWO

DEFEATING an almost overwhelming impulse to break into a run, Zanna walked briskly, head held high, round the turn in the lane. Once she was sure she was safely out of sight she slowed down, making herself breathe deeply in an attempt to regain her faltering composure.

This was the second time in a couple of hours that she'd been made to feel disconcerted and on edge. And she didn't like it, not one little bit.

Just what I needed, she thought with angry irony. A garage hand with attitude. The ideal end to a perfect day.

And she was determined it would be the end. She was already deeply regretting this sentimental detour. As soon as the car was fixed she would be off back to her city centre hotel and its mechanical civilities. At least she knew what to expect there.

However, the village, when reached, was certainly charming. The cottages which lined the road were stone-built, many with thatched roofs and gardens bright with seasonal flowers. Aubretia tumbled in shades of purple and crimson over low front walls, and laburnum and lilac trees were already heavy with blossom.

The road itself led straight to the broad expanse of the village green. Apart from a railed-off cricket square in the middle, it was tenanted solely by a pair of tethered goats, who lifted their heads from their grazing to watch Zanna curiously.

She hesitated in turn, wondering what to do first and feeling ridiculously conspicuous.

On the face of it, there was no one else around.

Emplesham seemed to be drowsing in the sunlight. But Zanna sensed, all the same, that from behind the discreetly curtained windows of the clustering cottages her arrival had been noted.

She decided, for reasons she could barely explain to herself, not to pinpoint Church House immediately. She'd behave like any other tourist who'd stumbled in off the beaten track. She was here, ostensibly, to look at an art exhibition, and that was what she would do.

The green was bordered on three sides, she saw, by more houses, a shop-cum-post office, a pub—whose sign announced it as the Black Bull and offered real ale, meals and accommodation—and the church, rising like a stately and benign presence behind its tall yew hedge. Apart from a narrow track beside the churchyard, which presumably led to the farm mentioned by her persecutor, there was no other visible egress.

The village hall stood on the opposite side of the green to the church, a wooden board fixed to its railings advertising the exhibition.

Zanna found herself in a small vestibule, where a woman in a flowered dress, seated behind a table, paused in her knitting to sell her an exhibition catalogue for fifty pence.

'You're just in time.' Her smile was friendly. 'The show ends today and we'll soon be clearing the hall for tonight's dance.'

'Dance?' Zanna's brows lifted. Far from being asleep, Emplesham seemed to be the Las Vegas of the neighbourhood, she thought caustically.

'Oh, yes,' the woman said cheerfully. 'It's become an annual event. We combine the art club's exhibition with the church's spring flower festival and make it a real celebration.' She nodded towards the double doors leading into the hall. 'I hope you enjoy the show—although there isn't a great deal left for sale, I'm afraid.'

'It really doesn't matter,' Zanna assured her politely. 'I'll just enjoy looking round,' she added, not altogether truthfully.

Nothing, however, could have prepared her for the riot of colour and vibrancy which assaulted her senses inside the hall. Every possible hanging space was filled, and by work which was a thousand miles from the pallid watercolours and stolidly amateurish still-lifes she'd been expecting.

Landscapes in storm and sunlight seemed to leap off their canvases at her as she trod cautiously round. She could almost imagine she could smell the scent of the grass and trees, feel on her face the wind that drove the heavy clouds.

There was a life section too, depicted robustly and without sentimentality, and, of course, the paintings of fruit and flowers which she'd been anticipating. But even here she was surprised, realising that she could almost taste the sharpness of the green apples arranged on that copper dish, that if she reached out a hand she might draw blood on the thorns of the full-blown roses spilling out of that jug. She would, she realised, have bought either of them—only they were already sold.

How in the world, she asked herself bewilderedly, could people in this small country district have learned to paint with such passionate exuberance? She found herself, absurdly, wanting to cheer.

One canvas stood alone on an easel towards the rear of the hall, as if deliberately set apart from the rest.

As she approached it the breath caught in Zanna's throat. She thought, I don't believe this—I don't...

But she knew she wasn't mistaken. The long, low house, hung with wisteria, bathed in sunlight, looked serenely back at her, just as it did in her precious photographs. Only the child playing in the garden was missing.

But her imagination could supply that, Zanna thought, exultantly noting that there was no red dot to say the painting was sold. In spite of everything, she'd been meant to come here. It was going to be a perfect day after all.

'Do you need any help?' The woman in the flowered dress had come up behind her.

'I was looking at this.' Zanna tried to sound casual. 'I can't find it in the catalogue, but I suppose it's a local scene?'

The woman laughed. 'Very much so. It's the house across the green, next to the church. And it hasn't been listed because it's only on loan, I'm afraid.'

'On loan.' Zanna felt sick with disappointment.

The woman nodded. 'It belongs to Mr Gordon, who actually owns Church House.'

'I see.' Zanna heard the despondency in her own voice and rallied, biting her lip.

What's the matter with you? You bought Zolto Electronics this morning, she scolded herself. Why be so easily put off over an oil painting? Everything's ultimately for sale, if the price is right.

Her mouth stretched in a smile Henry Walton might have recognised. 'Well, perhaps he might consider a private offer.'

'I hardly think so.' The woman gave her an astonished look.

'All the same, I'll call round and ask,' Zanna said with a shrug. 'Nothing ventured, nothing gained.'

'But Mr Gordon isn't here.' A swift frown drew the woman's brows together. 'He spends most of the year abroad.' She spread her hands in a gesture that was half-helpless, half-affronted. 'You'd really be wasting your time in pursuing this.'

'You're probably right,' Zanna said quickly as the woman turned away. 'It's just such a beautiful house. Has this Mr Gordon had it long? Do you know anything about the previous owners?'

There was a brief silence, then, 'I believe the house passed through a number of hands before the present purchase was completed,' the woman returned frostily. 'I'm sorry I can't be of more assistance.' And she walked away.

Visitors to Emplesham were apparently tolerated but not encouraged to push their luck by asking too many questions, Zanna thought ruefully as she followed the stiff figure out of the hall.

With a brief word of thanks, curtly acknowledged, she went out into the sunshine.

Occupied or not, Church House drew her across the green like a magnet. And this time she didn't care who might be watching.

The gate opened noiselessly under her hand. A mossy path led between smoothly trimmed lawns to the front door. Apart from pigeons cooing in the neighbouring churchyard, and the hum of a bee roving in the flowering tub beside the door, everything was still.

It was as if the house were waiting for her, she thought, her heart thudding painfully in her chest. As if all she had to do was lift the heavy wrought-iron knocker and the door would open and she would be drawn inside.

But to find what? She didn't even know, she acknowledged with a sigh.

Besides, all that really lay behind the half-closed curtains was someone else's home. And a very elegant home too, from what she could glimpse, with expensive chintz, oak beams and the gleam of well-polished furniture not from this century.

He might be an absentee, but Mr Gordon was a careful owner, she thought. The house and garden were both being maintained in pristine condition, which gave their emptiness almost an air of pathos. Or was that simply what she wanted to think?

Sharply aware that she had no right to be prying in this way, but unable to resist the temptation, Zanna followed the path round to the rear of the house.

The kitchen window was rather more revealing. She could see a massive Welsh dresser, laden with blue and white china, an Aga, with a row of copper pans suspended above it, and a big farmhouse table with a bowl of fruit at its centre.

Also, she realised in shock, a used mug and plate, together with assorted crockery, and, pushed to one side, an upturned loaf on a chopping board, a butter dish and a pot of honey, as if someone had eaten a hasty breakfast and left without clearing away the traces.

Yet the house was supposed to be empty. Surely not squatters, she thought, dismayed, and then yelped in fright as a hand descended on her shoulder.

'Having a good look round?' enquired an all too familiar drawl.

Zanna swallowed hard before turning. 'What are you doing here?'

'I told you I'd find you.' He gave her that hooded look. 'Although you do turn up in some surprising places. Are you just a snoop, or do you housebreak on the side?'

Zanna was furious to find she was blushing to the roots of her hair.

'Please don't be ridiculous,' she said, dragging the

remnants of her dignity around her. 'The house seemed—empty. I thought it might be for sale.'

'And you plan to make an offer they can't refuse?' He shook his head. 'You're going to be unlucky. I can promise you it's not on the market.'

'I'd prefer to discuss this with the owner.' Zanna lifted her chin.

'Who's in America.'

'Well, someone's living there.'

He slanted a glance towards the window and the betraying clutter inside. 'Yes,' he said slowly. 'There's a resident caretaker.'

'Good. Then he'll be able to give me Mr Gordon's address.' She put a snap of emphasis on the name.

'You have been busy.' The dark eyes looked her thoughtfully up and down. 'But you've got a fair wait ahead of you. He has a day job.'

'Oh.' Zanna bit her lip.

He was still watching her. 'However, if you really want to meet him, he'll be at the dance tonight.'

'The dance?' she repeated with amused incredulity. 'I don't intend to hang around that long.'

'You may have to,' he said laconically. 'You seem to have picked up some dirt in your petrol. I need to strip down the carburettor.'

'Hell's bells,' Zanna muttered. 'How long is that going to take?'

There was a pause, then, 'It'll be ready in the morning.'

'Oh.' Zanna made no attempt to hide her dismay. She wanted to abandon this ridiculous trip down Memory Lane and get back to civilisation. 'You couldn't possibly finish it tonight?' she urged.

'I'm sorry.' His tone held no regret at all that she could hear. 'You see, I'm going to the dance.'

'But of course.' She glared at him. 'Please, don't allow my convenience to stand in the way of your social engagements.'

'Don't worry, I shan't.' He actually had the nerve to grin at her. 'I suggest you book a room at the Black Bull. Tell Trudy that I sent you.'

'Thank you.' Her voice froze. 'I'm sure I can manage without your assistance.'

'Fine.' He turned to leave. 'Just don't offer to buy the place,' he tossed back at her over his shoulder. 'It's been in the family for generations.'

Zanna, standing rigidly, waiting for the click of the gate to confirm his departure, realised with shock that her hands had clenched tautly into fists.

What the hell was the matter with her? She could handle a boardroom full of angry men, so how was it this—this peasant could get under her skin so easily?

Because I allowed it, she admitted with angry bewilderment. It's almost as if I've been bewitched since I got here. First the car—now me.

She snorted with self-derision and began to walk slowly back to the front of the house.

She had come to Emplesham to see her mother's old home, and all she'd achieved was an odd feeling of dissatisfaction, bordering almost on desolation.

Yet what had she really expected? To step back in some time-warp and find Susan Westcott waiting for her? Surely she wasn't such a fool.

Maybe the lesson she'd come here to learn was that she'd gain nothing by raking over the past. Perhaps that was why her father had stripped himself of all reminders of his brief marriage.

Just as soon as the car's fixed I'm out of here, she promised herself grimly. And without a backward glance either.

* * *

Trudy Sharman was a large, smiling woman, with grey-ing blonde hair pinned into an untidy knot on top of her head.

'A room for the night's no problem. The tourist season hasn't started properly yet.' She nibbled the end of her pen. 'But I can only offer you a restricted menu for dinner. You see…'

'Everyone's going to the dance,' Zanna supplied re-signedly.

Mrs Sharman laughed. 'Well, yes. My husband's doing the bar and I'm catering. We won't be getting much trade here, so we've given most of the staff the night off.' She sent Zanna a faintly anxious glance. 'I'm sure it's not what you're used to.'

'It'll be fine.' Zanna made herself smile reassuringly. 'I'll have some sandwiches in my room and an early night.'

'Oh, we can do better than that.' Mrs Sharman looked scandalised. 'I said ''restricted'' not ''non-existent''. There's beef and mushroom casserole, lamb cutlets, or I can recommend the fish pie. And you'll be coming to the dance, surely?'

Zanna shook her head. 'I—I don't dance. And, any-way, I'm hardly dressed for a social occasion. But the fish pie would be lovely,' she added brightly.

'Shall we say seven o'clock, then?' Mrs Sharman se-lected a key from the row of hooks behind her desk. 'Just in case you change your mind about the dance,' she added vaguely.

Zanna bit back a sharp retort and followed her upstairs in silence. She had to admit, however, that her room was charming, with the blue and white sprigged pattern on the wallpaper repeated in the curtains and frilled bed-cover. The bathroom was only tiny, but well equipped. A small wicker basket on a table beside the bath offered a tempting range of soaps, scented bath oils and shampoos, and there was a courtesy robe in dark blue towelling hanging behind the door.

Zanna found it all totally irresistible. As soon as she was alone she filled the deep tub with steaming water, added jasmine oil, pulled off her clothes and sank gratefully into the luxurious perfumed depths, feeling the tensions ease out of her.

When she'd finished soaking, she used the hand-spray to shampoo her hair, then, wrapped in the towelling robe, rinsed out her scraps of silky underwear and hung them on the heated rail to dry.

Then she stretched out on the bed and reached for the telephone. First she rang the Grand Vista hotel, directing them to hold her room for two more nights, then called her own answering machine to see if there were any messages.

Her father's voice, irritable and slightly hectoring, was on the line. 'Zanna? Where are you? What the devil are you playing at? Call me back at once—d'you hear, my girl?'

To hear was normally to obey, Zanna realised as she replaced the receiver. But not this evening. Maybe not even tomorrow. Just for once she was off the hook, and she intended to enjoy the sensation for as long as possible.

There was a selection of books on the night-table, including—joy of joys—a Dick Francis she hadn't read.

That's my company for the evening sorted out, she thought with satisfaction, instantly closing her mind against the sudden intrusive image of a dark, mocking face and a pair of hooded eyes.

What on earth is the matter with me? she asked herself, in profound irritation. And couldn't find an answer that gave her any satisfaction at all.

By the time her dinner was served her hair was dry, and so was her underwear. She redressed herself reluctantly, longing for a change of clothes, then brushed her hair severely off her face, confining it with a ribbon in its usual style before descending to the bar.

To her surprise she found it quite crowded, with cheerful, chattering people clearly there for pre-dance drinks. But a swift, wary glance told her that her *bête noire* was not among them.

When it was her turn to be served, she ordered a dry sherry.

'Trudy's laid your table in the snug,' the barmaid told her, carefully handing her a brimming schooner. 'She thought it would be a bit quieter in there.'

Zanna carried her drink through the doorway indicated. It was a small room, cosy, with high-backed settles and polished oak tables. A small fire of sweet-smelling apple logs had been kindled in the hearth, dispelling the faint chill of the evening.

Only one table was laid for a meal, but two places had been set, with a bowl of freesias and a single candle burning in a stylish glass holder. There was, moreover, a bottle of Chablis waiting in a cooler.

Zanna, viewing these preparations in total bewilderment, heard the door squeak open behind her—presumably to admit Mrs Sharman with her meal.

'There's been some mistake,' she began. 'I didn't order any wine...'

'It's a peace-offering.'

The voice she knew at once. Only too well. But as she swung round to face him, her expression freezing into annoyance, a surprised gasp escaped her parted lips rather than the haughty dismissal she'd been framing.

Clean-shaven, with that dark mane of hair neatly combed, he looked almost prepossessing. His clothes—

the well-fitting dark trousers, the pale grey jacket that might almost be cashmere, the classic white shirt and the silk tie in sombre jewel colours—all bore the hall-marks of Italian designer wear. And the aroma of engine oil had been exchanged for the discreet scent of a very up-market cologne.

In fact, more than prepossessing, she realised with shock, as a strange awareness shivered along her nerve-endings. He was dangerously attractive.

That faintly mocking grin hadn't changed, however. And Zanna had noticed before what beautiful teeth he had.

'Lost for words?' he enquired lightly. 'That must be a novelty.'

'Well, yes.' Zanna drew a breath. 'I—I hardly recognised you,' she added lamely.

'Perhaps that's not such a bad thing.' He paused, as if choosing his words carefully, his face suddenly serious. 'I think we got off on the wrong foot earlier.' He gestured towards the table. 'I'd like to make amends.'

She felt her heart thump painfully, as if in warning. 'That's really not necessary.'

'You're condemning me to eat alone in the opposite corner?' There was a smile behind the plaintive words. 'I was thinking of Trudy as well, you see,' he went on beguilingly. 'How much easier it would be for her if we shared a table.'

Somehow he made it sound all so reasonable—so impossible to refuse.

Without quite knowing how, Zanna found herself facing him across the freesias. And, as if at some unseen signal, Mrs Sharman bustled in with the first course.

Their meal began with watercress soup, served with a swirl of cream. Zanna had thought she would have no appetite, but she finished every drop.

'Good?' her companion queried, with a smile across the flickering candle-flame.

'Better than that.' Zanna put down her spoon with a sigh. 'I was expecting just fish pie.'

'Not from Trudy's kitchen. Even though it's officially closed tonight she has her pride, and you're a resident so must therefore be cherished.'

'And what's your excuse?'

He shrugged. 'I'm a lonely bachelor who has to forage for himself, so she takes pity on me once in a while.'

If he was lonely, Zanna thought wryly, then it had to be through his own choice. Or perhaps he was simply too busy trying to maintain a small business to organise a private life as well.

That was something she could understand. She'd acted as hostess for her father times without number, but she couldn't remember, she thought with bewilderment, the last time she had dined *à deux* with a man.

Few, if any, of the men who'd sought her company had passed muster after Sir Gerald's rigorous vetting.

'You're my daughter, Zanna,' her father had constantly reminded her. 'My heiress. How can you ever be sure if it's you they want or my money?'

It was a lesson which had gone home, however much it might have hurt.

But this time there was no real risk involved, she assured herself. Because the man facing her across the table had no idea who or what she was. And she firmly intended to keep it that way.

As if picking up some unspoken cue, he said, 'We've never actually introduced ourselves, have we?'

'No.' Zanna's mind worked quickly. 'I'm Susan,' she announced. 'Susan—er—Smith.'

'Really?' The firm mouth quirked slightly. 'How unusual. And I'm Jake.' He paused. 'Jake—er—Brown,' he added, with sardonic emphasis.

Zanna felt her cheeks pinken, but she made herself meet his glance with apparent unconcern. After all, what did it matter? she comforted herself. They were ships passing in the night. Nothing more. And she had no more wish to know his real identity than to reveal her own.

The arrival of the next course relieved the awkwardness of the moment. The fish pie more than lived up to its recommendation. Under its creamy mashed potato and cheese topping, cod, smoked haddock and prawns jostled for precedence in a delicious creamy sauce, and then, to finish with, there was a sumptuously rich chocolate mousse with a wicked undercurrent of brandy.

Jake led the conversation throughout the meal, but he kept to general topics, touching lightly on places of interest in the locality and leading on to the success of the exhibition. Nothing on a personal level, she noted with relief.

Finally Trudy brought excellent coffee and a smooth Armagnac.

Who could ask for anything more? Zanna wondered as she leaned against the high back of the wooden settle, cradling the goblet in her hand and contemplating the flames leaping around the sweet apple logs.

'Don't get too comfortable.' His smile reached her across the candle-flame, sending a faint, troublous shiver down her spine. 'I'm claiming the first waltz.'

She sat up with a startled jerk. 'But I'm not going to the dance.'

'Why not? There's nothing else to do tonight.'

'I don't dance.'

'I'll teach you.'

'And I'm not dressed for it,' she added swiftly.

'You could be—with a few adjustments.' He rose and came round the table to her side.

Stunned, Zanna felt him release the ribbon holding her hair.

'Now that is so much better,' he said softly as the blonde strands fell forward to curve round her face.

He reached down, almost in the same movement, and undid the top button of her blouse.

Her hand lifted swiftly to check him as the blood stormed into her face. 'What the hell do you think you're doing?'

'Only this.' With total insouciance he tied the ribbon round her exposed throat in a neat bow, then lifted her to her feet, making her face the mirror over the fireplace. 'So, Cinderella, you shall go to the ball.'

Unwillingly, Zanna looked at herself. Her cheeks were still flushed and her eyes looked twice their normal size. Against her throat, the dark band of ribbon was a perfect foil for her creamy skin, while the neckline of her blouse revealed a tantalising glimpse of cleavage.

I look different, she thought with bewilderment. I don't know myself.

In the mirror's reflection, their eyes met.

He said softly, 'Tell me, Miss Smith, does anyone ever call you Susie?'

She shook her head, the loosened hair swinging against her cheek. 'Never.' The word seemed squeezed from her taut throat.

'Then tonight they will.' His gaze held hers, steadily, almost mesmerically. Somehow she could not break the spell and look away, much as she wanted to. Much as she needed to. 'Dance with me, Susie—please?'

She searched wildly for the crushing retort, the ulti-mate put-down that would salvage this ridiculous—this impossible situation. And instead heard herself say, against reason, against wisdom, even against sanity, 'Yes.'

CHAPTER THREE

ALL the way across the green, Zanna could hardly believe that she was doing this.

I make my own plans, she thought. I'm the one in control. So how the hell am I on my way to some village hop, with a rustic grease monkey who has far too much to say for himself?

And who, whether she wished to acknowledge it or not, had far more than his fair share of sexual charisma, a voice in her head warned acerbically.

The kind of man that Suzannah Westcott would have shunned by miles.

But tonight, just for a few hours, she was leaving Zanna Westcott behind her. She was going to be Susie Smith instead, and find out, maybe, how the other half lived. And where was the harm in that? she argued with herself as she looked up at the velvety sky.

With the man walking at her side, that was where, returned the voice in her head, which refused, stubbornly and annoyingly, to go away.

Above the dark roofs the stars seemed close enough to touch, and a sliver of new moon was peeping round the church tower. Ahead of them, the hall was festooned with coloured lights, and music drifted on the faint breeze.

It was, to all intents and purposes, a night for lovers, she thought with unease. And if Jake had tried to take her hand, or put an arm round her waist, she knew she would have turned tail and fled back to the sanctuary of her solitary room at the pub. But he didn't attempt even the most casual physical contact. For which, she told herself firmly, she was sincerely thankful.

And then they were inside the hall and people were calling greetings, their welcoming smiles mixed with friendly speculation as they looked at Zanna, and imperceptibly she began to relax. After all, she reasoned, there couldn't be much danger in a room full of other people.

She hardly recognised the hall itself. In the space of a few hours all traces of the exhibition had been removed and the entire room decorated with more lights and swathes of silk flowers. Tables and chairs had been set out round the perimeter of the dance floor, and a three-piece band was playing on the platform.

It was like stepping back through a time-warp into another era—another planet, she thought, staring round her.

'What were you expecting—the latest disco sounds?' He didn't miss a thing.

'No—oh, no,' she denied hastily. 'It's—quite a transformation, that's all.'

Jake's brows rose. 'Then you did come to see the exhibition?' He sounded surprised.

'Of course,' she countered lightly. 'What else?'

He shrugged. Suddenly that hooded look was back. 'I was hoping you'd tell me.' He paused. 'Did you actually buy any paintings?'

'No—the one I wanted wasn't for sale.' She hadn't meant to say that, she thought with vexation, and went on hurriedly, 'In fact, most of them had been sold. The standard of work is absolutely amazing for such a small village. They must have a very good teacher.'

'Several, I believe.' His tone was almost dismissive. 'They also have a drama group, a gardening club and a choir, so you won't go short on cultural activities.'

'I won't?' She looked up at him, puzzled, and saw his mouth slant in a grin.

'When you come to live here,' he explained gently. 'I thought you were planning to buy a house?'

'Well, yes.' She could have kicked herself. 'But I gathered I was on a hiding to nothing over that.'

Jake shrugged again. 'I suppose there's always a chance—if you make the right offer,' he returned. 'As I said, the caretaker for Church House will be around later. You could always have a word with him. See how the land lies.'

'Thank you, I certainly will.' She made herself speak casually. 'Is there some kind of local history group in the village, by any chance? I'd like to get to know a little more about the place before making any firm decision, you understand?'

'Oh, yes,' he said slowly. 'I understand perfectly.' He paused. 'I'll gladly introduce you to a few people, but I can't guarantee they'll tell you what you want to know.'

'Just some general background would be fine,' Zanna declared airily, and untruthfully. And someone who knew a child—a little girl called Susan. Someone to fill in some of the aching blanks in her own childhood.

The tempo of the music changed, became slower, more dreamy.

'This is our waltz.' Jake held out a hand, inviting her to join him on the dance floor. Zanna hung back, shaking her head, aware, suddenly, that her pulses had begun to thud erratically.

'I really don't dance.'

'Didn't you have lessons at your exclusive boarding school?' he drawled.

'Well—yes,' she conceded reluctantly. 'But that was a long time ago.'

'Then it's time your memory was jogged.' She was

drawn firmly and relentlessly into his arms. 'I lead—you follow.'

Which wasn't a situation she was used to, as he was probably well aware, she thought, gritting her teeth. For the first few moments she felt totally awkward, her feet everywhere, her body stiff and unyielding in his embrace. But gradually she found herself responding to the rhythm of the music, as well as to her partner's unspoken signals, as he guided her round the crowded floor.

As the final chords sounded she said stiltedly, 'Thank you, I enjoyed that.'

'All you need is more practice.'

'I don't think I know any dance teachers.'

'Not at waltzing, Susie,' he said quietly. 'At living.'

There was a brief, startled pause, then she said thickly, 'You have a hell of a nerve.'

'Famous for it,' he agreed, without any visible signs of remorse.

'Damn you—I have a very good life.'

'Crammed with all kinds of goodies, I have no doubt,' Jake said expressionlessly. 'But that isn't what I mean.'

Zanna lifted her chin, giving him a look that had originated well north of the Arctic Circle.

She said, coolly and precisely, 'You may be well-versed in the inner workings of motor vehicles—although that has still to be proved—Mr—er...'

'Jones,' he supplied cordially. 'As in *Alias Smith and*...'

Zanna bit her lip hard. That was not the name he'd given previously, she thought thunderously, but it seemed wiser, under the circumstances, to ignore it rather than call the matter into question.

'But I suggest you lay off the human psychology,' she went on, raising her voice a semitone. 'At that you're a total amateur.'

'As I imagine you are yourself, Susie. At least at the things that matter.' He gave her an edged grin. 'Now let's go and get some drinks.'

'No, thanks,' Zanna refused curtly. 'I think I'd rather go back to the Black Bull.'

He had the audacity to laugh. 'Don't sulk.' And, as her lips parted in furious negation, he added, 'And don't fib either. Just think of what Reverend Mother would have said.'

'How did you know I went to a convent?' she demanded suspiciously.

His smile widened. 'Call it a lucky guess.' He paused. 'Besides, if you run away now you could miss out on a guided tour of Church House. Isn't that worth enduring my company for a little while longer?'

He took her hand in his and led her round the edge of the floor to a room at the rear of the hall where the bar had been set up.

Bill Sharman was burly, with a beard and an infectious laugh.

'Now then, Jake,' he said jovially, giving Zanna an appraising look. 'What can I get you both?'

'A cold beer, please.' Jake turned a questioning eye on Zanna. 'The same for you, Susie?'

'I don't drink beer.' Nor did it seem politic to drink any more alcohol when she needed to keep her wits about her. Glancing round, she spotted with relief several large glass bowls, filled with some innocuous-looking ruby liquid and awash with sliced apples, pears and oranges, standing on a side-table. 'But I'll try the fruit cup,' she added, ladling some into a glass.

'A good choice,' Bill Sharman said cheerfully. 'Trudy's special brew. No dance here would be complete without it.' He paused. 'My wife tells me you're spending the night with us.'

'Yes, it wasn't exactly a planned visit, but my car broke down and it's taking Jake longer to fix it than I'd hoped.'

There was an odd silence, then Bill said, 'Ah, you'll be old friends, then?'

To her surprise, she found herself flushing. 'Not really. I...'

'Actually, we only met this afternoon when she walked into the garage.' Jake broke smoothly into her flustered words. 'And as she was at a loose end tonight I invited her here.'

'Splendid,' Bill approved, almost too heartily. 'Great stuff. Have a wonderful evening.'

'Thank you.' She smiled back at him. 'And the fruit cup is delicious.'

It was, too, the flavours of the fruit mingling coolly and fragrantly with a hint of spice. Cinnamon? she wondered as she sipped again. And nutmeg, perhaps? It was difficult to tell, she decided, downing some more in the interests of scientific research.

Jake took the glass from her hand and placed it with his own on a convenient window-ledge.

'Come and dance,' he invited softly.

This time it was a slow foxtrot, and Zanna was astonished to find how quickly she picked up the steps. She was almost sorry when the tempo changed completely to a rollicking Gay Gordons, a progressive version, where she found herself being whirled round by a succession of different partners, leaving her laughing and breathless as the music ended with a triumphant flourish.

She looked instinctively to see where Jake was and saw him standing at the side of the dance floor, talking to a pretty redhead who was openly and unashamedly devouring him with her eyes.

Which was fine by her, thought Zanna, swallowing

the remains of her fruit cup and starting back to the bar in search of a refill. Of course it was. Jake belonged to Emplesham, after all. He had a life here which would continue long after she was gone and forgotten.

A strange pang of something like regret assailed her at this thought, and was instantly suppressed.

Because she had a life too. A very different life from those led in this backwater, she told herself robustly. A life where she was needed—where she mattered.

She pinned on a resolute smile for Bill Sharman. 'Dancing's thirsty work,' she said, plying the ladle.

'Always was,' he agreed, raising one eyebrow. 'Take it easy if you're not used to it.'

'I'm fine,' she returned airily. 'Having the time of my life.'

Which, somehow, did not include watching Jake being eaten alive by pretty girls with red hair. An unwelcome realisation if ever there was one.

Dismissing it, she held out some money for her drink, but Bill shook his head.

'That's our contribution to the festivities—Trudy's and mine. There's no charge.'

They'd opened one of the side-doors, and she stepped through it and out into the cool darkness, fresh with the scent of newly mown grass. She stood, sipping her drink and looking up at the sky.

The new moon was still there, a pale silver crescent above the trees. The breeze lifted her loosened hair, brushing it against her cheek, the nape of her neck, like a caressing hand.

She moved uneasily, aware that she was shivering— not with cold but with a strange, unfathomable excitement.

You could wish on the moon, she thought hazily, re-membering the old childish superstition. And if you turned a piece of silver over in your hand and bowed three times your wish would come true. But she had nothing to wish for.

And she knew, even as the thought took shape in her mind, that she was lying to herself.

She recognised with sudden, shocking clarity exactly what she would wish for—if only she dared…

She thought, I want this night never to end. I want to go on being Susie. I want…

And she stopped there, her mind closing against the unspoken, unutterable plea. All the breath seemed to leave her body in one gigantic, soundless gasp. She could feel the coins clenched in her hand, biting into her flesh.

The temptation to turn them over, to obey the ritual and accept whatever fate decreed would follow, was almost overwhelming.

Almost—but not quite. From some corner of her mind a remnant of sanity intervened to save her, reminding her precisely who she was and what, in fact, he was.

A total stranger, she thought stonily, gulping the sweetness and the pain of the night back into her starved lungs. A stranger, moreover, light years removed from her in background and aspiration. Someone she wouldn't have given a second glance to in her busy London existence. Someone she'd been unwise to allow anywhere near her. Someone already well aware of the effect he had on women, as his redheaded admirer could probably attest.

She gave the moon one last look. You pathetic fool, she told herself savagely, and she turned to go back into the hall.

Only to yelp in fright as she cannoned into a tall figure standing behind her.

He steadied her without particular gentleness. 'This is

getting to be a habit. What the hell are you doing out here?'

'Moongazing,' she said. Her voice sounded odd, as though it didn't belong to her. 'I—I needed some fresh air.'

'Trudy's punch tends to have that effect,' he said grimly. 'Bill told me you'd been back for seconds.' He took the empty glass from her hand and shook his head. 'This stuff should carry a government health warning. Not to mention all the other things you drank during dinner.'

Zanna stiffened. 'I hope you're not implying…'

'I'm stating a fact.' His arm was like a band of steel round her waist as he guided her back into the hall. 'From now on it's orange juice for you, Susie, if you want to be fit to drive in the morning.'

She hung back, glaring at him. 'Maybe I should just go back to the Black Bull and sleep it off.'

He snorted impatiently. 'You're really keen to be on your own again, aren't you?'

No, she thought. Suddenly I'm not any more, and it scares me. I want to feel safe again—self-sufficient and safe—like I did yesterday, and all the days before that.

Aloud, she said stiltedly, 'Look, I'm sure you had plans for tonight—people you wanted to meet here.' She could see the redheaded girl watching them avidly from the other side of the room. 'I must be spoiling things for you. If you'll just introduce me to this caretaker friend of yours, I can leave you to enjoy your evening.'

He looked at her for a moment, his brows drawn together in a frown, then he sighed abruptly. 'Don't run out on me, Susie. At least, not yet.'

The music had started again, another slow, beguiling waltz, and before she could think of a viable excuse Jake had swung her effortlessly into his arms and back onto the floor.

'Relax,' he said laconically into her ear as she stiffened. 'Stop fighting me—and the world.'

His arms tightened, drawing her close against him. She felt the warmth of him penetrating through the layers of clothing to her own skin and beyond. Felt the frozen, frightened core hidden deep within her begin, unbelievably, to dissolve away, leaving something unknown, new and vulnerable in its place.

She knew that she should not—could not allow this to happen. That suddenly the danger she'd sensed was all around her, pressing on her, and that she had no one but herself to blame.

She knew also, and more disturbingly, that she wanted to press closer still. To bury her flushed face in the curve of his shoulder and breathe the unique male scent of him. To feel the harsh pressure of his lean, muscular body against her breasts, her belly, her thighs. To spread her hands against the powerful breadth of his back and reach up to touch the thick silky hair curling gently at the nape of his neck. To feel his mouth touching hers.

The need was bone-deep and desperate, but she knew she had to fight it if she was going to walk away from him tomorrow unscathed. As she had to do, she reminded herself.

She said, with a little nervous laugh, 'Actually, you could be right about the alcohol. I—I didn't realise. Maybe I should go back and sleep it off. As I have to drive tomorrow.'

There was a silence, then he said levelly, 'Fine. I'll get your jacket.'

Having him walk her back across the moonlit green wasn't part of the plan at all.

She hung back. 'I hardly need an escort. There can't be many hidden perils in this village.'

'Who can tell?' His tone was brusque. 'Anyway, I'm not prepared to take the risk.'

But the risk was all hers, Zanna thought numbly as he helped her on with her jacket. And the only real danger was right here beside her. Because no amount of punch, however lethal, could account for the way her blood seemed to sing in her veins, for the throbbing awareness of every sense, every nerve-ending in her body, as they started out through the scented darkness together.

She stumbled on a tussock of grass and instantly his arm went round her. 'Careful.'

'Oh, hell, my shoe's come off.' She scrambled frantically round with a stockinged foot.

'And it's not even midnight yet.' There was amusement in his voice. 'Keep still, Cinderella, and I'll see if I can find it.'

'We need a torch.' Standing on one leg made Zanna feel undignified as well as giddy.

'Something Prince Charming lacked too.' Jake came back to her side. 'I'll continue the search later, when I have one, Susie. But in the meantime...'

Before she could utter a word of protest, he swung her up into his arms as easily as if she were a featherweight and carried her across the grass.

When she could speak, she said icily, 'Put me down, please.'

He lowered her to the ground with almost insulting promptness. 'Are you planning to hop the rest of the way?'

'Of course not,' she snapped, angrily aware of her racing pulses.

'Then stop turning a problem into a crisis.' He picked her up again, without ceremony, and set off.

'You think you have an answer for everything,' she said bitterly.

'I often wish I had.' She felt him lean forward to release the catch on a gate and looked round in swift alarm.

'But this isn't the Black Bull.'

'Full marks for observation, Susie.' He carried her up the path, then deposited her gently on the mat while he reached into his pocket for some keys. 'You did say you wanted to look round Church House? Well, now's your chance.'

'But what right have you...?' Her voice trailed away into stunned silence. Then, 'My God,' she said slowly. 'It's been you all the time, hasn't it? You're the care-taker. You've just been stringing me along all evening.' She shook her head. 'Oh, I don't believe it.'

'I hope,' he said, gravely, 'that you're not going to reproach me, my dear Miss Smith, for not being entirely honest with you?'

His words seemed to hang in the air like a warning as he pushed open the front door, and turned to her. 'Would you like me to lift you over the threshold?'

'No, I wouldn't,' Zanna said stormily. 'I'd like to go back to the inn.'

'And so you shall.' His voice was almost soothing as he urged her into the hallway. 'Just as soon as we've had some coffee.'

'I don't want any bloody coffee.'

'Well, I do, so tough.' He opened a door, switched on lights, and Zanna found the house taking shape, coming to life before her just as she'd always imagined. In spite of herself she felt interest, excitement building inside her.

'And I'd take off that other shoe,' Jake added over his shoulder, walking into the kitchen. 'You don't want a sprained ankle to add to your other woes.'

'At least you admit they exist.'

'I imagine I'm responsible for most of them—in your eyes anyway.' He filled a kettle and set it on the Aga to boil. 'And while we're on the subject I may as well confess that I finished your car this afternoon. It's working perfectly again and I parked it at the Bull before I met you for dinner.'

Zanna stared at him, shoe in hand, momentarily mute with outrage. But only momentarily. 'Why the hell didn't you tell me this earlier?'

'Because I had this perverse compulsion to dance with you, Susie. To see you smile. To discover if there was a softer layer under all that autocracy and aggression.'

'Don't think I'm flattered by your interest,' she almost spat back at him. 'I presume, now that you're curiosity's been satisfied, I'm free to get out of this dump?'

'Not immediately.' He collected pottery mugs from the dresser and spooned coffee into them. 'Unless, of course, you actually want to lose your licence?'

The fact that his comment was quite justified did not improve Zanna's temper.

'That's none of your concern,' she said curtly. 'And you had no right to deceive me.'

Jake's brows lifted. 'Which particular deception did you have in mind?'

'And don't laugh at me,' she flared.

He shook his head. 'I'd sooner weep.'

And so, she discovered to her horror, would she. The tears were there, just below the surface, threatening to destroy her. And she could not afford to humiliate herself in front of him. Could not allow herself to give way to such appalling weakness.

'The kettle will be a minute or two.' His voice broke the sudden tense silence. 'I'll use the time to find your other shoe.' He paused. 'If you want to look round the house, do so. I give you the freedom of the place.'

'Do the owners know that you do this?' she demanded raggedly. 'That you allow complete strangers to—to invade their privacy in this way?'

'You won't find any dark secrets or no-go areas.' Jake took down a powerful flashlight from a shelf near the back door. 'And you're only a stranger if you want to be.'

'You know nothing about me,' she argued stubbornly. 'I could be a thief.'

His smile glinted as he glanced at her stockinged feet. 'How far do you think you could hobble with your ill-gotten gains? Besides,' he added, 'I already know you better than you think. And I intend to find out more.'

His glance locked with hers, watching enigmatically as her eyes dilated in swift shock, as she tried and failed to look away. The air between them was suddenly charged, sparking with a new and dangerous tension.

When she spoke, her voice, to her own ears, seemed to come from some far distance. 'And what exactly do you hope to discover?'

He said, quite gently, 'Everything, Susie. Every last living thing. Because, I warn you, I won't be satisfied with less.'

And he went out into the darkness, leaving her staring after him in something very close to panic.

CHAPTER FOUR

FOR a while Zanna sat where she was, rigidly still, her hands twisted tautly in her lap. That was how he would find her when he returned, she told herself. Unmoving and unmoved.

And just as soon as she had her shoes back she would put a stop to the whole farcical situation and leave.

But as the stillness of the house settled round her like a warm cloak she found herself imperceptibly beginning to relax. She started to allow herself to look around and assimilate her surroundings.

It was very much a working kitchen, she realised. The copper pans bore all the marks of long service, a fearsome array of well-used utensils hung on butcher's hooks from a wrought-iron carousel and the thick wooden chopping block was grooved with use.

A far cry from the clinical atmosphere of her own kitchen in London, she thought wryly, where the only device in constant use was the microwave.

Eventually, drawn by a compulsion deeper than mere curiosity, she got up and went out into the hall.

The light was on in the drawing room, and the door stood invitingly open. It was a long, low room, its focal point a magnificent stone fireplace with a dog grate. The sofas and chairs were furnished with down cushions, thick enough to lose oneself in. Every table and cabinet gleamed with the loving sheen of polish, applied over many years.

The whole atmosphere of the room spoke of comfort

long-established, far transcending the gloss of mere luxury.

And above the fireplace the picture of Church House was hanging, drawing her forward almost magnetically, just as it had done at the exhibition.

'My picture,' she whispered.

For a long moment she stood, staring up at it, then turned away with a defeated shake of her head.

Someone else's picture, she told herself. Someone else's house. And even if I possessed them both, I would find no clues to tie them to the past.

But what had she really expected? Coming here had always been a fool's errand.

But—in for a penny, in for a pound, she thought with a shrug as she left the room. Her intention had been to return to the kitchen, but instead she found herself making for the broad oak staircase. Perhaps, once she had trodden every floorboard, seen every room, she would be able to exorcise the demons that drove her.

And one of those demons would soon be back, she realised with a faint shiver as she went swiftly and softly up the stairs.

She could neither explain nor excuse the strange effect that Jake seemed to have exerted on her. He was the last man in the world to have appealed to her in ordinary circumstances. Yet nothing that had happened since she arrived in Emplesham could be deemed ordinary.

It was if she had been bewitched—bound by some spell—as soon as she'd entered the village. As if she'd breached some unseen thicket of thorns to reach the lair of the enchanter.

And who knew what she might find up here, behind these discreetly closed doors? No secrets, he'd said, but all the same she felt like Bluebeard's bride as she turned the first handle and looked in.

Prosaically, it was only the bathroom—but what a bathroom. It was decorated throughout in subtle shades of blue and green, with an enormous square sunken bath. Beautiful ceramic candleholders were stationed at each corner of the wide tiled surround, every one with its own tall, virgin candle.

To lie in the bath in the flicker of candlelight would be like swimming underwater through some warm, tropical lagoon, Zanna realised with a swift intake of breath.

The carpet under her feet felt soft, and as deep as the sea. Thick fluffy towels waited on the heated rails. The trace of some familiar scent hung in the warm, faintly moist air, and as she sniffed experimentally she recognised Jake's cologne.

Well, naturally, she told herself dismissively. He was living in the house. He would use the bathroom. The absence of wet towels on the floor, or traces of shaving soap on the basin and mirror, revealed, too, that he was personally fastidious. But why should he be a slob just because he repaired cars for a living? she reproved herself.

He was, after all, a stranger. She didn't even know his real name—any more than he knew hers. So why should anything about him surprise or annoy or please her? She should aim for a calm indifference about every aspect of his life and personality.

Her eyes wandered back to the bath. Did he ever lie there, she wondered, her breathing quickening, with the candles lit, imagining he was floating on some balmy, moonlit sea? And did he lie there alone?

The image was suddenly too troublesome to contemplate, and she backed hurriedly out, pulling the door shut behind her, controlling the irritating flurry in her pulses before proceeding to the next closed door.

A bedroom, she discovered, furnished with the same

discreet comfort she'd noticed downstairs, the wide bed
covered with an old hand-made patchwork quilt. But no
actual sign of occupation.

A linen cupboard, a box room, another bedroom—this
time with a single bed, but again apparently unoccupied.
And behind a door at the far end of the passage a flight
of steep wooden steps. Leading perhaps to the servants'
quarters? Zanna wondered wryly as she made the cautious ascent.

But it wasn't a bedroom at all that awaited her. A
faint evocative aroma of oil paint and turpentine reached
her, as well as a sudden chill. Zanna looked up and
found the moon looking back at her. For a crazy moment
she thought she had somehow walked out into the open
air, before she realised that almost half the roof had been
replaced by an enormous skylight. A studio, she thought.
My God, it's an artist's studio. And maybe the very
place where the picture of this house was painted.

Her fingers fumbled for the light switch. She felt as
if she was on the brink of some genuine revelation. But
as the light came on she saw, with swift disappointment,
that the studio which had indeed been created here under
the rafters was almost bare. An easel was folded against
a wall and in the corner a draughtsman's chest stood
with open, empty drawers. Palettes and brushes, all immaculately cleaned, were ranged on a table. Beside
them, a tray held half-used tubes of paint.

Whoever had worked in this room had clearly not
been there for some time. It was all too orderly—too
blank. There wasn't even a discarded sketch to provide
the connection she needed.

Sighing, Zanna turned off the light, and retreated back
down to the landing.

One more room to go, and that, presumably, would

be the master bedroom. Surely Jake couldn't be using that?

But one glance told her she was wrong. The discarded shirt lying across a chair, the brush, comb and toiletries jostling on the dressing table and, most tellingly, the deep red coverlet, matching the canopy of the massive four-poster bed and folded neatly back at the bed's foot—all these shouted his occupation.

For a mere caretaker, he certainly took a hell of a lot for granted.

But she could understand his choice. It was, undeniably, a beautiful room, with the glowing colour of the bed-hangings matched by the twining crimson roses on the thick carpet.

She had seen all there was to see up here. Now she should close the door and go back to the kitchen before Jake returned. Yet, inexplicably, Zanna found herself drawn forward, her feet sinking into the carpet as she crossed the room. The satin-covered quilt felt as soft as thistledown under her questing fingers while the sheets and pillowcases were in cool ivory percale. She touched them too, smoothing the palms of her hands over the rounded surfaces of the pillows.

His skin would look like burnished bronze against them, she thought bemusedly. And if she bent closer, put her cheek there also, and her lips—like this—she would breathe the scent of him, as if she were lying in his arms.

The sheer enormity of what she was thinking—what she was doing—what she was actually desiring—exploded suddenly in her head. She straightened, recoiled as if jerked on wires. Her hands flew to her mouth, as if wiping away a touch—a kiss. In the startling silence she could hear the hoarseness of her own breathing.

She had to break the spell of this dangerous enchantment, she told herself feverishly. She'd taken too many risks already. Now she had to get away—to escape without looking back.

On her way to the door she caught a brief glimpse of herself in the dressing table mirror. With her dishevelled hair, unbuttoned shirt and the dark ribbon round her throat, she was barely recognisable as the girl who'd entered her hotel suite in triumph only hours before. Now, with her bright, startled eyes, and the feverish spots of colour burning in her cheeks, she looked like some wild creature of old—some maenad off to a dark and secret revel.

Out of character, she thought, and out of control. She snatched off the ribbon, stuffing it into her jacket pocket, then hastily ran her fingers through her hair, trying to subdue it to a semblance of normality. She would not, she thought, under any circumstances use Jake's comb.

With one final, almost despairing look at her reflection, she turned and plunged out onto the landing. She was panting when she reached the head of the stairs— where she halted, all the breath leaving her body in one silent, tumultuous gasp of shock.

'Enjoy the tour?'

She hadn't heard a sound in those last bewildered, bewitched minutes, but he was back just the same, standing with one foot on the bottom stair, resting an arm on the banister, totally at his ease.

A faint smile played about his mouth as he looked up at her, but the dark eyes were hooded, enigmatic.

She had the curious, appalling sensation that he knew, somehow, where she had just come from. That through doors and walls he had seen that humiliating performance by his bedside.

Desperately she rallied her tottering defences. 'It

was—instructive,' she returned coolly. 'Tell me, do your employers know that you sleep in their bed?'

His grin widened. 'They probably guess.' He hunched an indolent shoulder. 'I like plenty of space, Susie.'

Innocuous words, on the face of it, but they conjured up a whole torrent of images, each more disturbing than the last. To her horror, Zanna felt an involuntary blush rising.

She stayed where she was. 'Did you find my shoe?'

'I did, Cinderella, and it still isn't even midnight.'

'Don't be absurd,' she said shortly. 'In fact, this whole ludicrous situation has gone quite far enough. I'd like to leave, please.'

The smile still lingered. 'That's entirely your own decision, Susie. However, you'll still need your shoe.'

He turned away and walked across the hall into the drawing room, leaving her with no choice but to follow.

In the doorway she halted, her eyes widening. 'What on earth's this?'

A fire had been kindled in the grate, and one of the tables drawn up to the small blaze. A number of plates had been set out on it. Astonished, Zanna recognised vol-au vents and slices of quiche, rolls of pink ham stuffed with asparagus, chicken drumsticks, small bowls of different salads and a stick of crusty bread.

She looked at Jake, who was filling mugs from a cafetière. 'A little something you ran up in a spare moment?'

He shook his head. 'I'm only responsible for the coffee. The rest is Trudy's idea. We left the dance before supper, you see,' he added, deadpan. 'So she packed up our share in case prolonged fasting made us ill.'

'She can't be serious,' Zanna said faintly. 'I've barely recovered from dinner.'

'She's a born provider. You can't possibly hurt her

and refuse to try at least a mouthful.' He paused. 'She also sent you this.' He held up a key. 'It opens the side door at the Bull, in case there's no one around when you go back there.'

'Oh.' Zanna digested this. 'Well, that was—thoughtful.'

'She always is.' Jake put down the cafetière. 'Why don't you stop hovering and sit down?'

'Because I'm not staying.' She held out a resolute hand. 'If I could have the key, please, and my shoes, I'll be on my way.' She encountered the measuring look he sent her and lifted her chin. 'It's getting late and I have an early start tomorrow.'

'You have a long drive ahead of you?'

The question was casually put, but Zanna stiffened. This was straying onto forbidden territory.

'Does it matter?' She let her hand fall to her side.

'Probably not.' His smile was easy. 'But, like you, Susie, I have an outsize bump of curiosity. And, as you must be aware by now, you intrigue me.'

She gave a brittle laugh. 'Do you regard everyone whose car breaks down in the same light?'

'Hardly.' The look that lingered over her from the top of her head to her slender feet was still amused, but frankly and disturbingly sensual at the same time.

'And while we're on the subject of cars,' Zanna babbled on, bitterly aware that her betraying blush was persecuting her again, 'perhaps you'd tell me how much I owe you for fixing mine?'

'We can discuss that,' he said, 'over supper. So, take a seat and drink your coffee.'

There was a seething pause. Then, 'You really like your own way, don't you?' Zanna snapped.

'I'd say that was something we shared,' Jake retorted

equably. 'Now, are you going to sit down of your own accord, or do I have to fetch you?'

Zanna sent him a fulminating look, then, head held high, marched to the sofa and sat down on its edge. 'Satisfied?'

'Far from it.' Maintaining a careful distance between them, Jake put the coffee down on a side-table within her reach. 'But the night is young.'

'Does it ever occur to you,' Zanna said through gritted teeth, 'that your attitude could be construed as sexual harassment?'

'Not often.' He sent her an oblique glance. 'I'm an old-fashioned man, darling. I know exactly how the human race has kept going over the centuries, and it's not through any strict adherence to political correctness, believe me.

'Besides,' he added coolly, 'apart from a few cherished moments, your own attitude has been nothing to write home about. I'll swap my sexual harassment for your sheer bloody aggravation any old time, and call us quits.'

'Then I wonder you're so damned keen to keep me here,' Zanna flashed.

'I'm also an optimist,' Jake drawled. 'Maybe I'm hoping for a few more moments to cherish.'

She said tersely, 'Don't hold your breath.' Then she glanced at the plate of food he'd set beside the coffee beaker. 'And I really don't want anything to eat.'

That much was true anyway, she thought. Her stomach was churning. Every nerve-ending in her body felt as if it were stretched on wires.

'Try your coffee, at least.' Jake took the sofa on the opposite side of the hearth, stretching out his long legs. He'd discarded his jacket already, loosening his tie and casually undoing the top buttons of his shirt. Now he unfastened his cuffs, rolling back his shirt-sleeves to reveal muscular forearms with a faint dusting of dark hair.

His voice reached her, edged with amusement. 'I said, do you want some cream?'

She hadn't heard because she'd been too busy watching him instead, she thought with vexation.

Forcing composure, she shook her head. 'I'll take it black.'

It was the right decision, she realised after the first cautious sip. Jake's brew was scaldingly hot, strong and delicious.

She needed something to counter the effects of the alcohol—especially that lethal punch. She hardly drank at all under normal circumstances, and she simply wasn't used to it. That was the real—the only explanation for her pathetic and totally uncharacteristic behaviour.

And if this doesn't bring me to my senses, she told herself wryly, savouring the dark, aromatic liquid, then maybe nothing will.

'Are you cold?' His abrupt question broke the silence between them, making Zanna realise that she had unconsciously stretched out a foot towards the fire.

'Not really.' She pulled a small face. 'Just making the most of real flames while I have the chance. Central heating is efficient but impersonal.'

'A great many things are,' he agreed drily. He reached for his jacket, extracting a high-heeled shoe from each pocket. 'You'd better have these back now.' He crossed to her and dropped on one knee. 'I'll put them on for you.'

She fought the impulse to shrink back in her seat and won. 'I can manage.'

'No one could doubt it.' There was an edge to his voice as his hand closed on her ankle, gently but firmly. 'But this is my pleasure.'

Zanna sat mute and like a statue as he fitted first one shoe then the other onto her outraged feet.

'Thank you,' she said icily when he'd finished. 'If the garage business ever fails, you could always get a job as a shoe salesman.'

'Relying on you for a reference? I don't think so.' Jake sat back on his heels, contemplating his handiwork. 'I'll just stick to Plan A and marry a rich woman.'

The breath caught in Zanna's throat. 'An admirable ambition,' she said at last. 'Is there a village organisation to cover that as well?'

'We have our fair share of lonely hearts.'

'Including the pretty redhead at the dance?' The question must have been there, lurking just below the surface, all the time, but she could have bitten out her tongue just the same.

'That'll be the day,' he returned cheerfully, without the barbed comment she'd been dreading. 'Sal's a party girl.'

She shrugged. 'Even party girls settle down eventually.'

'But not with me.'

'Not rich enough?'

'I'll check her bank balance and let you know.'

'Not very gallant.' She made her tone light, slightly waspish, trying to conceal the fact that he was still physically far too close for comfort. She was piercingly aware of the lean, graceful strength of his body, of the shadowing of body hair tantalisingly visible through the thin shirt, and that faint, evocative fragrance of cologne.

She hurried into speech again. 'I was sure I'd spotted the future Mrs Smith.'

'Wrong on several counts, Susie. Including the name. You're Smith, if you remember. I'm...' He paused.

'Yes?' she said. 'Exactly what are you?'

'Call me X—the unknown factor.' He glanced up at her, not smiling now, the dark gaze intent. 'So, tell me about him, Susie. Tell me about the man who's made you so uptight.'

There was a brief silence, then, 'There is no man,' she said jerkily.

Jake shook his head, holding her glance with his. 'I don't believe that. You're a beautiful, desirable girl, but you've fastened yourself into some kind of cage. And I want to know why.'

'You're being totally absurd again.' Zanna's voice rose angrily. 'You know nothing about me. And you haven't the slightest right to make these assumptions.'

'Maybe not, but that isn't going to stop me. Do you plan to spend the rest of your life with iron bars around you? And what are they for anyway? To keep you in or the rest of the world out?'

'I have a very good life,' she said raggedly. 'I'm free to go where I want and do what I wish. A freedom I intend to exercise now, incidentally.' She rose determinedly. 'I'd like that key, please. I'm going back to the Black Bull.'

Jake got lithely to his feet. He took the key from his pocket and stood for a moment, tossing it in his hand, his expression speculative.

'I'm waiting,' Zanna said icily.

'Which will do you no harm at all.' The dark eyes flashed at her. 'Or do they all jump to attention in the big wide world when you look and speak like that?'

'Until I came here I was treated with the respect I've earned,' she said stonily. Apart from this morning, came the unbidden thought, when Henry Walton looked at you as if you were dirt.

'But at what cost to yourself, Susie?'

It was the sudden gentleness in his voice which proved her undoing.

Her throat tightened uncontrollably. She said in a muffled voice, 'Oh—go to hell,' and burst into tears.

From some place of stark and desperate loneliness she felt his arms enclose her. Her hands reached for his shoulders, clutching them as if he were a rock in a stormy sea. Sobs were torn out of her from some aching depth she had not known existed. She was blinded and deafened by the force of her own emotions. Dimly she was aware of being lifted—held, rocked and soothed as if she were a child again.

Not the child she'd actually been, the bewildered thought came to her, but a child who was allowed to be hurt, to be vulnerable, to show pain like other children. A child who was allowed to fail, who had the right to be comforted.

A child who was a stranger. And Zanna wept for that strangeness.

Yet slowly, gradually, the tempest of tears began to ebb. Her body might still be shaken by long, quivering sobs, but control was returning. And full awareness.

She was on the sofa, held closely in Jake's arms, cradled across his thighs. Her wet face was pressed against the curve of his throat and his hand was stroking her hair.

'Oh, God.' Confused, she tried to sit up—to disentangle herself. 'I—I'm sorry…'

'Relax.' He made no attempt to release her, his hand gently urging her head back to its former resting place. 'You don't have to apologise.'

'But I don't understand.' There was a catch in her voice. 'I've never behaved like this before.'

'I guessed that already.' His tone was wry. 'You don't have to explain either. Or be afraid. You're safe.'

Safe? she thought. Safe? With a man who called himself X, the unknown factor? There was no safety here. Especially when the warmth of his body seemed to be invading every fibre of her being, tempting her to stay where she was, enticing her to turn her head and press her mouth to his skin. To feel the strong pulse in his throat beating against her lips, finding its echo in the surge of her own blood.

But that was sheer insanity, and she knew it. And prudence insisted that she distance herself from him without delay.

Only, detaching yourself and sitting up with dignity on a man's lap had its own inherent problems, she discovered. Especially when you were trembling so much inside you felt as if you might shatter into a million tiny pieces at any moment.

'Will you let me go, please?' She'd intended that to sound positive and self-possessed. Instead it had sounded more like a dying wish, she realised, vexed.

He said, slowly, 'Any form of intimacy really bothers you, doesn't it?'

'No, of course not.' She tried to laugh. 'I'm just— seriously embarrassed by all this. I don't know what can have come over me.'

'You came into contact with real life.' He shrugged, and the slight movement of his body against hers sent a disturbing tremor through her senses. 'And your protective shell wasn't as strong as you thought.'

'You really think you have me all worked out,' she said bitterly.

Jake shook his head. 'No, Susie. I suspect that would take a lifetime.'

'Well, my life is all worked out, thanks.' She drew a deep breath. 'And now I really do have to go.'

'We still,' he said, 'have to discuss my fee for the work on your car.'

'Yes, of course.' She tried swiftly to reckon how much cash there was in her wallet. Under normal circumstances she'd have paid by cheque or credit card, but they had her real name emblazoned on them. And she was determined not to reveal that. Nor must she forget that there'd be a bill from Trudy Sharman to settle too, she reminded herself with faint dismay. She rallied herself.

'How much do I owe you?' she asked, aiming for her old briskness.

'One kiss,' he said softly. 'And we'll consider the matter settled.'

'*What?*' she almost shrieked. Outrage provided the impetus she needed and she leapt to her feet, glaring at him. 'That is a disgusting suggestion.'

Jake shrugged again. He looked totally relaxed, completely unabashed by her reaction.

'OK,' he said equably. 'Two hundred pounds.'

Zanna froze. 'That is a joke, I hope.'

'It was a fiddly, time-consuming job,' he said. 'Labour is costly, especially when it includes call-out fees, overtime—and a percentage for aggravation,' he added gently. 'Maybe you should have asked for an estimate before I began.'

'You can't possibly justify such an amount,' she protested angrily.

'I don't have to. It was an emergency job, according to you, and that's the price I'm charging for it. Unless, of course, you want to reconsider the alternative,' he added meditatively.

The silence between them was suddenly electric, crackling with tension.

'You must be mad,' she said finally, unevenly. 'Two hundred pounds—for a kiss?'

'Why not? It will be worth every penny to taste you, Susie—to touch that delectable mouth you keep so tightly buttoned and find out if, somewhere, there's honey beneath the acid.' He shook his head again. 'I don't think there's a man born who could resist such a challenge.'

His slow smile reached out and touched her, reawakening the inner trembling, the strange, enervating weakness which seemed to pervade her body when their eyes met.

'After all,' he added softly, 'what's a kiss between friends?'

What, indeed? It was ridiculous that her heart should be pounding like this. She'd been kissed before, for heaven's sake. But not often, and admittedly not well. Usually a brief, embarrassed brushing of the lips that signified thanks after dinner or a visit to the theatre or cinema. Thanks and generally goodbye.

This, if she permitted it, should be no different. A way of extricating herself. A final conclusion to a bewildering episode. The full-stop at the end of the sentence, that was all.

So why should she be so sure that if she allowed Jake to possess her mouth, even for an instant, life would never be the same again?

He stood up slowly, still holding her gaze with his.

'Kiss me, Susie.'

His voice seemed to reach her from a far distance. And yet he was so near—so close.

Close enough to touch, was her last coherent thought as she stepped forward into his arms, lifting her face to his like a flower turning to the sun.

CHAPTER FIVE

HIS mouth was cool and very gentle as it began its slow, lingering exploration of hers.

Somehow she had always known it would be like that, she realised in quiet bewilderment. As if in some strange way this was the moment she'd been created for.

She stood pliantly in the circle of his arms, aware that every fibre of her being was awakening and responding to each new sensation that his caress engendered. She felt his tongue trace the firm contour of her upper lip, his teeth tug softly at the quivering fullness of the lower one, trembled as kisses like the brush of silk touched each blunt, vulnerable corner of her mouth. And as the pressure of those kisses gradually deepened into sensuous insistence.

And then mere acceptance was no longer enough, either for him, or, she recognised with shock, for her. Her head fell helplessly back, like a rose too heavy for its stem. Tiny stars danced behind her closed lids as her shaking hands reached up to fasten round his neck and draw him closer still, while her lips parted, sighing, to answer his demand.

Their mouths locked in a possession that was also a surrender. A ravishment that was also a gift. Zanna fed on him greedily, the breath moaning softly in her throat, driven by desire for the first time in her life, deaf to everything but the thunder in her blood.

She thought, in some reeling corner of her mind, I never knew. Dear God—I never knew...

They swayed together blindly, oblivious to everything

but this hunger, this mutual, overwhelming need that seemed to be consuming them both.

Her body strained forward, urging against him in an instinct as old as time, carrying her over some dark and irrevocable threshold.

She was aware of him caressing her—of his hands stroking her small high breasts, teasing the nipples to vibrant, startled life, then gliding down over the curves and planes of waist, stomach and hips to the soft, guarded cleft of her thighs.

She heard herself gasp in shock, and in a pleasure that was almost guilt at his touch.

He said huskily, 'Look at me, Susie. I need to see your eyes.' And then as she obeyed dazedly, 'Has there been—anyone for you? I have to know.'

'No.' The denial was a thread of sound as she stared up at him from under weighted lids. There was a pause, then he nodded, slowly. His face looked stark, pared down to bronze angles. A flush burned along the high cheekbones and the dark gaze seemed to simmer into hers for one endless, stinging moment...

Then, without another word, he lifted her into his arms, cradling her head against the hard curve of his shoulder, and carried her out of the room and up the stairs.

He put her on the bed and lay beside her, propping himself on one elbow as his eyes searched her face. He touched her cheek with his hand, then followed the outline of her throat down to the opening of her shirt. Where he paused.

'Now,' he said softly, holding her gaze with his. 'Now let us find out what we both enjoy.'

He kissed her again, his mouth moving on hers lightly and sensuously, and began to unfasten her clothing as delicately and unhurriedly as if he were parting the petals of a flower. As he slipped the lacy cups of her bra away from her breasts her hands lifted instinctively, to cover herself, but he stopped her, catching her wrists and holding them prisoner.

'Don't hide yourself,' he whispered. 'There's nothing to be afraid of. Don't you know how lovely you are?'

The dark head bent over her and she felt his lips on her skin, his tongue drawing lazy circles around the dark pink areolae before taking each dusky, sensitised bud fully into his mouth.

Her whole body shuddered at the sensation, half in shock, half in a pleasure that edged on pain, as she entered the unknown labyrinth of her own sexuality.

His hands moved on her, uncovering her, discovering her until she was naked in his arms. Dazed with kisses, quivering in response to every movement of his caressing hands, Zanna only became aware that he too had stripped when she felt the erotic friction of his hair-roughened skin against her silkier flesh—a new delight that she accepted raptly, running her hands across his shoulders and down the supple spine, making him half-gasp, half-laugh.

His hands were tracing patterns on her skin, marking out a path for his lips to follow, over the slight concavity of her stomach to the slender pelvic bones and downwards. Heartstoppingly and inevitably downwards. And when, at last, his languorous exploration attained the ultimate intimacy, the long, experienced fingers finding the moist sweetness of her hidden self, she sighed, arching her back luxuriously against his questing hand, her hips moving restlessly in search of a surcease as yet unguessed at.

'Soon,' he whispered against her mouth. 'Soon, I promise.'

His hand moved rhythmically, tantalising, arousing

the tiny satin pinnacle of her desire with swift, deft strokes.

Zanna's breathing tautened—quickened. Her head twisted wildly on the pillow as her self-control slid away. Her whole being seemed turned inwards, focused solely on the piercing sweetness of the sensations Jake was creating in her, on the silken spiral of tension carrying her further and further to some undreamed-of height—some uncharted realm of pleasure.

When the moment of release came at last she heard herself cry out as her body trembled into spasm after spasm of aching rapture and then, finally, was still.

When she could again think coherently she realised there were tears on her face, and she tried to turn away, ashamed of her weakness, aware that this was the second time she'd wept in front of him tonight.

'Susie.' His voice was very tender. He captured her chin, making her face him, then leaned forward, kissing away the salty drops.

'I'm sorry,' she said huskily. 'I never cry...'

'You mustn't reject emotion,' he said quietly. 'Or be ashamed of it either. And that was quite a lot to assimilate—for a first time.'

He took her in his arms and held her, stroking her hair, the curve of her shoulder, until her breathing steadied.

'Now tell me,' he said. 'Why did you cry? And I want the truth.'

She didn't meet his gaze directly. 'Because it was so beautiful,' she answered at last, a slight catch in her voice. 'And then it was—over.'

'Not at all.' There was a smile in his voice. 'That, my lovely one, was only the very beginning.' He took her hand, placed a kiss on its smooth palm, and carried it to his body. 'You see, Susie,' he whispered, 'you're allowed to touch me too.'

She said uncertainly. 'You mean that's what you want—all you want?'

'Oh, no,' he told her softly. 'I don't mean that at all. As I shall soon make more than clear. You see, my sweet, I suspect that your capacity for pleasure is greater than you could ever have dreamed.'

Her voice was uneven. 'You don't know. You don't understand…'

'But you're wrong.' His hands were gentle as he drew her to him, his voice little more than a murmur. 'So wrong.'

His mouth on hers was a flame now, warming her, reviving her. Under his silent urging she began to explore his body in turn, savouring with renewed hunger the hidden strength of bone and muscle. At his loins she hesitated, her fingers shy at first as she clasped him, encircled him. His swift, involuntary groan of pleasure drew her on, filled her with unfamiliar daring. She was entranced by his delight—by the sense of power it bestowed. Tonight she was learning her own womanhood—realising what it meant to be desired, and, with increasing insistence, to desire.

His hands were on her breasts again, making them bloom and swell in excitement as his fingertips teased her flesh. His mouth found hers again, his tongue flickering across her parted lips before seeking and exploring the moist depths. A mirror image and a promise, she realised hungrily, of other delights soon to follow.

She was molten with longing, stricken to the heart with the need he was arousing in her.

And, in recognition of its mutuality, she felt the graze of his thigh between hers as he raised himself over her and then, with one fluid, silken thrust, entered her.

For one moment in time she was mute, motionless, her eyes widening endlessly as she stared up at him, assimilating the reality of his possession, the actual physical sensation of holding him, enclosed within her.

Then, quite simply, in total acceptance, complete surrender, she lifted herself against him—and gasped at his instant, unequivocal response.

They moved together in a kind of controlled frenzy, mouths locked together, sweat mingling as their bodies twisted in heated, endless demand. As if, Zanna thought, in one coherent corner of her reeling mind, this were the sole reason for their creation. This glorious, voracious, burning urgency driving them relentlessly on to some undreamed of culmination.

When their climax was reached, Zanna felt as if she were being torn apart, body and soul. Every sensation was so acute, she thought she might die of pleasure. From some distant place she heard Jake cry out, his voice hoarse, almost unrecognisable.

They drifted back to earth, and a kind of sanity, still close in each other's arms.

When she could speak, Zanna said huskily, 'Is it—always like that?'

'No.' The negation was shaken, almost curt. His body was still joined to hers, his head heavy against the curve of her shoulder. She touched the tangle of his dampened hair and, smiling, drifted into sleep.

She woke to his kiss. Her lids lifted slowly, languidly, to find him bending over her. She smiled up at him and slid a hand between the lapels of the towelling robe he was wearing.

Jake captured her straying fingers and kissed them. 'Presently.' His voice—the look in his eyes—promised other yet-undreamed-of delights, and she shivered, but not with cold, as he drew back the covers.

He held out a robe that matched his own. 'Now I have a surprise for you, Susie.'

He led her out of the room and along the landing. The bathroom door was open, and a warm breath of roses and jasmine drifted on the air.

Zanna caught her breath. The bath had been filled with gently steaming water, and flames like captive stars burned on the tall candles lit round its edge. There was also an ice bucket, she realised, chilling champagne and two glasses.

She said on a little gurgle of amusement mixed with an odd shyness, 'It looks like the setting for a Roman orgy.'

'Fine.' He loosened the sash on his robe and dropped it casually to the floor before sliding hers from her shoulders. 'I'll be Antony if you'll be Cleopatra. Sorry there's no asses' milk, but they don't deliver at weekends.'

It wasn't much of a joke, but she was grateful for it, their shared laughter easing the way for her into this new and unexpected level of intimacy.

She lay back in the scented water, supported by the curve of his arm, and drank the wine he'd poured for her, feeling the bubbles tingle in her head, knowing that she must be dreaming—except that even in her wildest dreams she'd never devised anything like this.

And when the glass was empty, and he took it from her hand, she leaned back against the padded headrest, her smile a frank invitation, and heard his breath catch, saw his eyes darken with purpose.

And then...

'No one's washed me since I was a baby,' she protested, half seriously, as he began very gently to massage soap into her skin.

'Then you've missed out badly.' He applied a dab of lather to the tip of her nose, and, with more minute attention, to each nipple. Her body clenched deliciously at his touch, and his slow smile told her that he was totally aware of her reaction. She looked into his eyes and saw the dazzle of the candle-flame reflected there. She leaned forward and kissed his lips.

His hands moved on her, caressing her softly, like the rippling of the water against her body, his touch expressing his delight and his growing need. A need that she shared.

Their coming together was almost leisurely, a slow, lingering enfolding. Zanna felt almost weightless in his arms, her hair floating on the water like a mermaid's as she surrendered herself. And at first the pleasure was gentle too, like the advance and reluctant ebb of a midsummer tide. Until, suddenly, the seeking became urgent, the swift ferocity of desire carrying them away, overwhelming them so that they were drowning in each other, mouths frantic, arms and legs entwined as their bodies strove for satiation.

And then the final wave lifted them, engulfed them, and threw them, gasping and crying out, onto a shore where, dazed and shaken, they found a kind of peace waiting for them.

She awoke slowly, and lay, momentarily disorientated, staring around her. Then sat up abruptly, in something close to panic, as she registered the unfamiliar room, the rumpled bed—and her own nakedness. And, most salient of all, the body of the man beside her, totally relaxed in deep, unmoving sleep.

For a moment she was completely still herself, gazing down at him as the first shock waves began to resound through her mind. And as she began to remember in detail a wave of shamed, incredulous heat swept through her body.

Was it possible that she—Zanna Westcott—had really allowed this to happen? That the cool shell she'd built around herself and believed to be impregnable had been so easily shattered—and by a stranger, at that. A man she'd only just met and certainly had no reason to trust. A village mechanic, for heaven's sake—a caretaker to whom she wouldn't have given a second thought in normal circumstances.

Dear God, she thought, swallowing. I must have gone mad.

But ever since she'd come to this place, she seemed to have lost touch with reality, she reminded herself, as if she'd been bewitched, held in the toils of some spell. Or was she simply making excuses for her own inexplicable, unforgivable loss of control?

Whatever, she was awake now, and back in her right mind. And her overriding need was to get out of this bed, out of this house and safely away before he woke too.

Slowly, and with immense care, she began to ease herself towards the edge of the bed, her eyes raking the room for her clothes. They seemed to be all there, littered jarringly across the carpet, apart from her jacket, bag and shoes, which were still downstairs, if yet another appalling memory served her correctly.

Zanna collected her things together, one frightened eye fixed on the bed and its occupant still, thankfully, dead to the world.

Please, she prayed silently, let me get out of here. Let me not have to face him.

The phrase 'in the cold light of day' had suddenly assumed a new and terrifying meaning.

The bedroom door opened noiselessly under her hand.

She'd intended to dress in the bathroom, but the evocative scent of bath oil, mixed with the more acrid odour of candle-wax stopped her in her tracks on the threshold.

No, she couldn't go back in there, she realised. The memories it aroused were too new, too raw—too potent to bear. She huddled into her clothes on the landing, then tiptoed down the stairs, listening intently for sounds of movement from the bedroom she'd just left.

But her luck seemed to be holding. As she retrieved the rest of her belongings and let herself out by the back door the house remained shrouded in silence.

Of course, it was still very early. There was no one immediately visible as she gingerly unlocked the side door at the Black Bull and let herself in, although she could hear the distant sound of voices and a clatter of crockery from the kitchen regions.

Just in time, she thought, going up the stairs two at a time, praying she wouldn't meet Trudy Sharman on the way. Her room was just as she'd left it, and if her luck held nobody would ever realise she'd not spent the night there, she told herself as she rumpled the sheets and dented the pillow.

She combed her hair, pulling it back fiercely into its usual strict confinement at the nape of her neck, trying not to wince as she fastened the ribbon back where it belonged. Trying to forget how it had looked tied round her throat.

She splashed her face and hands with water, then applied a dusting of the solid make-up base she favoured. Lipstick in hand, she paused. Because her mouth looked different, pink and swollen beyond the constraint of its usual cool contours. Her eyes too were shadowed, looking back at her with a knowledge as old as time. A stranger's eyes, she thought as she replaced the lipstick, unused, in her bag. A stranger's face.

She left the room, and went downstairs.

'Your bill already?' Trudy Sharman sounded surprised and disappointed. 'But surely you'll have some breakfast? It is included in the price.'

Zanna shook her head. 'I need to make an early start. I have appointments today—people to see.'

That sounded like her usual confident tone, with no giveaway signs of the sick trembling inside her. The pub was up and running for the day now, and every time a door slammed or a footstep sounded Zanna was on tenterhooks, scared to look over her shoulder in case Jake was there. Watching her. Waiting for her.

She paid the ridiculously small amount requested with cash, thanked Mrs Sharman, said, mendaciously, that she'd been more than comfortable, and went out to her car, trying not to run.

Well, he said he'd fixed it, she rallied herself as she slid behind the wheel. Now she could only hope it was true.

She turned the key in the ignition, and the engine—the traitor—purred into instant life, just as if it had never been away.

It wasn't until the village sign had been passed and she was heading back to the motorway that Zanna realised she'd been holding her breath.

Now all she had to do was go back to the hotel and collect the rest of her belongings. Then she would do what she should have done in the first place and return to London.

She'd taken a step back into the past and it had proved a dangerous country. Her wild-goose chase had ended in disaster, and she couldn't pretend otherwise.

Jake had got her if not actually drunk at least the worse for alcohol, and seduced her. A sordid story, and hardly unique, but she could arrive at no other explanation for her total loss of control. Nor make any other excuse either.

But at least he doesn't know who I am, she placated herself.

Susie Smith had been left behind in Emplesham, sloughed off like an outgrown skin, and she should be grateful for that. Grateful that she could at least vanish without trace and without recriminations, that she could erase the last disastrous twelve hours as if they had never happened and resume her life as normal.

Or what passed for normality...

For one searing moment her mind was invaded by an image of Jake as she'd last seen him, the lithe body that had been the tender, passionate, untiring instrument of her pleasure, relaxed at last in exhausted slumber against the pale sheets.

They had stumbled back to bed, still wrapped in the huge fluffy bath sheets they'd used to dry each other in hushed and tender intimacy, and later made love again, she remembered, starting with laughter and champagne and ending in a kind of fierce, mindless desperation. As if they had both known it was the last time.

She imagined him waking—reaching for her and finding the bed empty beside him. And she felt her heart lurch in anguish and the car slow as her foot automatically reached for the brake.

After which he would no doubt shrug, write her off as the one that got away and resume his life too, she reminded herself in savage self-derision, accelerating away again with renewed determination. She wouldn't be missed for long. There would be the pretty redhead, or some other 'Susie' to console him.

She closed her ears to the small voice in her mind asking how she was going to find consolation.

I'm my father's daughter, she thought. I'll make out.

*   *   *

Further reminders that she was Gerald Westcott's daughter awaited her at the hotel. Having failed to find her at home, her father had left a number of increasingly brusque messages at reception.

'Sir Gerald was concerned that you could not be contacted yesterday evening, Miss Westcott,' the receptionist told her, her eyes sharp with curiosity.

Zanna smiled coolly, 'I've been visiting friends and decided to stay over.'

'But you'll be checking out today?' The girl was already looking for Zanna's account on the computer.

'No, in the morning.' Zanna returned, her tone clipped. 'In the meantime, please hold all calls.'

She turned away, biting her lip. Her defiant reaction had been instinctive, but probably unwise. After all, it had been the assumption that she existed only to dance to her father's tune which had originally led to this fiasco, she reflected bitterly as she rode up to her suite in the lift.

The impersonality of her surroundings, which had previously been an irritant, now seemed oddly comforting. A good place to lick her wounds and generally recover her composure, she told herself.

She stripped off her clothes, shivering at the beguiling fragrance of rose and jasmine still clinging to her skin, and took a shower, treating it as a ritual cleansing, washing away Jake—the memory, the scent, the touch of him—for ever.

After all, she could not allow one act of foolishness to colour her entire life, she thought angrily.

She put on her nightdress, climbed into the smooth, impeccably made bed, and fell asleep almost at once.

It was late afternoon when she woke. She sat up slowly, pushing her hair back from her face, trying to clear her head.

She'd get dressed, she thought, then order some tea from room service to revive her. And she wouldn't skulk in this room all evening either. She'd book a table in the restaurant. Take charge of her life again.

After she'd made the necessary calls, she chose a pair of smartly cut cream trousers from the small selection of clothes she'd brought with her, topping them with a silk shirt the colour of sapphire. Then she sat down at the dressing table and brushed her hair till it gleamed.

Her tea would be arriving at any moment, so she reached for her bag, searching for her coin purse in order to tip the waiter.

As soon as she opened the bag, she knew that something was wrong. The purse, her wallet and credit card folder were all there, together with the usual jumble of diary, tissues and keys, yet a familiar bulkiness was missing.

And then she saw the gaping pocket and her hand went to her throat. She said aloud, 'Oh, no—my photograph album.'

She turned the bag out onto the dressing table, scrabbling frantically through the jumble of contents, but the leather folder was nowhere to be seen.

She tried to think back—to decide when she'd had it last. She'd glanced through it in her room at the Black Bull before going down to dinner last night, but she'd zipped it safely away again. She could swear to it.

On the other hand, she couldn't remember feeling it there when she'd reached into her bag for her make-up, just before this morning's precipitate flight.

So she must have lost it either at the dance—or, more disturbingly, at the house. Whichever it was, it was gone for good. Because she could not—dared not—take the risk of going back to look for it.

Sudden defeated tears pricked at her eyes and were

fought back. Perhaps it was for the best, she thought as she slowly replaced her things in her bag. Perhaps it was time she cut her ties with the past.

And whatever spell had bound her to Emplesham, she thought sombrely, was now well and truly broken.

CHAPTER SIX

ZANNA arrived back at her flat the following afternoon. The red light was blinking furiously on her answering machine, but the only messages were from Sir Gerald. As she pressed the rewind button it occurred to her how pleasant it would have been to have found a call from someone else—a girlfriend, perhaps, suggesting a meal out or a visit to the cinema. The kind of normal weekend activity that most of her contemporaries enjoyed as a matter of course.

It brought home to her suddenly how isolated, and indeed how humdrum, her life usually was these days. Unless she dined with her father she generally ate alone, and spent at least part of her weekend working.

Just as she had this time, she realised with a grimace as she plugged her laptop into her main computer terminal to print off her report on the Zolto Electronics acquisition, written after her solitary meal the previous night.

Anyway, she'd been too busy lately to cultivate any close female friendships, she told herself defensively. At one time there'd been Clare Mayhew, her best friend at school. They'd gone to university together, and when Clare had begun work at a City office they'd seen each other regularly. But Clare was now Mrs Gregg, with a daughter of less than a year to occupy her, and their relationship had slipped into a kind of limbo.

Maybe that was my fault, Zanna thought, watching the pages of the report issuing smoothly from the printer. Perhaps I should have tried harder to keep the thing going, accepted the dinner invitations and put up with Clare's efforts to pair me off with Jack's various friends.

But at the time she'd felt impatient—resentful, even—that Clare should imagine there was anything lacking in Zanna's busy successful life which could be put right by one of those pleasant but uninspiring males.

What the hell was there about getting married that turned otherwise sensible women into such inveterate matchmakers? she wondered restlessly.

The report concluded, Zanna changed into leggings and a sweatshirt and concocted herself a snack meal from cheese, crackers and a tomato she found wilting in the salad drawer of the fridge.

She was halfway through it when her front door buzzer sounded an imperious summons.

Zanna took a deep breath as she unfastened the safety lock. Then, 'Come in, Father,' she invited calmly.

'I should damned well think so.' Gerald Westcott was an imposing man, his stature enhanced by his immaculately tailored dark suit. His naturally florid complexion was darker than usual as he surveyed his daughter. 'What kind of game is this, Zanna? Where have you been all weekend? Didn't those fools at the hotel pass on my messages?'

'In great detail.' Zanna gestured towards the newly filled cafetière. 'Would you like some coffee?'

'I'd like some answers,' her father said brusquely. 'What possessed you to simply—disappear like that? Didn't you realise I'd be wanting a full report on Friday's meeting?'

'Of course, and here it is.' Zanna passed him the file. 'As for my so-called disappearance, I thought I deserved a small break so I took one. And from now on I may take more. All work and no play, you know,' she added.

'I'm glad you feel you can afford the luxury,' Sir

Gerald said grimly, his disapproving glance dismissing her casual attire. 'But in future you'll kindly report to me first before vanishing into the blue, and let me know where you can be contacted in case of emergency.'

'I see.' Zanna refilled her cup meditatively. 'Well, I'm glad you weren't worried about me, Father.'

'Worried?' The heavy brows rose. 'Why should I be worried? You're a grown woman, perfectly capable of looking after yourself, although I admit I was surprised and shocked to find you could behave so irresponsibly. But you're back now, so we'll say no more about it. You did well with the Zolto Electronics deal.' He nodded at her. 'You drove a hard bargain. I'm proud of you.'

Words, Zanna realised, that would once have been music to her ears but which now left her unmoved— even slightly uncomfortable. Henry Walton's tired voice seemed to echo in her head. *You're your father's own daughter, Miss Westcott.*

She said quietly, 'I'm glad you're pleased.'

'Come into the office early tomorrow.' He tapped the file. 'We'll have breakfast together and discuss this in detail.' He nodded at her again and left, as abruptly as he'd arrived.

Leaving me with my orders, Zanna thought bleakly as the door slammed behind him. And the rest of the day to get through somehow, alone with my thoughts.

And she found herself shivering.

'Are you all right, Miss Westcott?'

Zanna, splashing cold water onto her face, turned with a start to find Tessa Lloyd watching her. Her lips tightened. The bout of nausea she'd just endured had been as swift as it had been violent, but she'd comforted herself with the thought that there was no one else around in the women's washroom to be aware of her discomfiture. Now it seemed she was wrong, and there had been a witness after all. Damn.

She straightened, uneasily conscious that the world was still tilting dizzily, and reached for the paper towels.

'I'm fine, thanks,' she lied, avoiding her pale, glassy-eyed reflection in the mirror. 'It must have been something I ate.'

Tessa Lloyd frowned. 'Not, I hope, in the executive dining room. Should I speak to the caterers?'

Zanna tossed the used towel into the bin. 'I threw up, Miss Lloyd,' she returned coolly. 'No need to launch a full-scale enquiry.'

'But—forgive me—it isn't the first time this week, is it?' The other woman gave her a sharp stare. 'Are you sure you wouldn't like to see the Company doctor?'

Zanna bit her lip, silently cursing the efficiency of the office grapevine. 'Quite certain. I really don't want to turn a tummy bug into a federal case. But I might go home,' she added, sounding more nonchalant than she felt. 'See if a day in bed will shake it off.'

Tessa Lloyd gave a thin smile. 'And avoid passing it round the office too. These things can spread so rapidly in air-conditioned buildings.'

'I think I can safely say it isn't Legionnaires' disease.' Zanna tried to keep her irritation in check. 'I'll finish dealing with my post first—if that's all right with you?'

'Of course.' Sarcasm clearly washed over the Tessa Lloyds of this world. 'Shall I tell Sir Gerald you're ill?'

'That won't be necessary,' Zanna said quickly. 'I'll be back at my desk tomorrow anyway.'

In the month since she'd 'played truant', in Sir Gerald's deliberately jocular phrase, she'd hardly been allowed out of her father's sight for a moment. The work had piled up on her desk, hardly allowing her time for thought, let alone recrimination. At the weekends her presence had been demanded as hostess at a series of business functions. The puppet, she thought ironically, was back, responding to every pull on the strings. Any hint that she was even marginally unwell was likely to launch a major enquiry, and that was the last thing she wanted.

Her legs felt wobbly as she made her way back to her office. Megan, her secretary, waiting there for her, gave her an uneasy sideways look as she entered.

No prizes for guessing how Tessa Lloyd came by her information, Zanna thought grimly as she seated herself at her desk. Maybe it was time she looked for an assistant with more discretion.

'Anything urgent?' She began to glance through the pile of mail.

'I don't think so, Miss Westcott.' Megan hesitated. 'One of them was marked "Personal" so I left it for you.'

'Oh?' Surprised, Zanna picked up the thick cream envelope with its elegantly lettered superscription "Miss Suzannah Westcott". It was odd to see her full name spelled out for once, clearly by someone who didn't know her very well, she thought, fighting another surge of queasiness. She slit open the envelope and extracted an embossed invitation card.

Her brows lifted. The pleasure of her company was requested at the London opening of the Lantrell Gallery.

'Lantrell,' she said aloud. 'Do we know them? Does Westcott Holdings sponsor them?'

'I don't think so, Miss Westcott. Shall I ring down to the PR section and ask?'

'Why not?' The opening, Zanna noted, was in a week's time. As Megan went into her own office to telephone she picked up her diary and began to leaf through it. It was probably some kind of marketing ploy, she thought dismissively, and almost certainly she wouldn't attend, but as someone had taken the trouble to invite her, she might as well mark down the date and time.

She was still sitting, staring at the diary, when Megan returned. 'We have no connection with them, Miss Westcott, but Lindsay's heard of them. She says there are Lantrell Galleries in New York and Los Angeles, as well as Madrid, Paris and Nice.' She sounded as if the information had been learned by heart. 'Apparently they specialise in traditional rather than contemporary art and sculpture.' She paused. 'Miss Westcott—are you all right? You've gone as white as a sheet.'

Her voice seemed to come from miles away. With a supreme effort, Zanna closed the diary and put it down.

'Actually, I feel pretty dire.' She was astonished at how normal her voice sounded. 'There's some dictation on the machine for you, Megan, which I'll sign tomorrow. I'm taking the rest of the day off.'

'Will you be all right to drive? Should I call a cab?' Megan was flustered and fluttering. Zanna Westcott hadn't taken time off for illness in living memory. Perhaps she was human after all.

'No, and please don't fuss.' Zanna tried to soften the abruptness of the words with a parody of a smile. 'I— I'll be as good as new in the morning.'

Please, she thought as she picked up her bag and walked to the door. Please let that be true.

Zanna had always loved the view from her living room window. Loved the stretch of the Thames and its busy traffic. Today she looked unseeingly at the sparkle of the sun on the river in the early light.

She'd hardly slept the previous night, her mind in turmoil, examining and rejecting the evidence, telling herself that yesterday's suspicion could not be true—that the test she'd conducted some fifteen minutes ago would justify her completely. Because anything else was unthinkable.

She glanced feverishly at her watch, willing the time to pass, counting the moments. Her feet felt leaden as she eventually crossed to the bedroom, and went into the bathroom beyond.

The mark on the test tube seemed to glare at her, confirming her worst nightmare.

Her clenched fist pressed against her abdomen. 'No,' she whispered in anguish. 'Oh, dear God, no.'

Had that one reckless night in all her careful life led so disastrously to this? Had it really happened? Could it be true?

Even with the incontrovertible proof in front of her, the questions—the denials beat in her brain.

She was Zanna Westcott. She didn't make mistakes. She thought things through. She considered the consequences and made balanced decisions.

Except once, when she'd allowed herself to be carried away on some private tide of madness. But now the tide had receded, she thought savagely, leaving her marooned on some desperate and lonely shore, more frightened than she had ever been in her life.

The walls of the bathroom seemed to be closing in on her. She almost ran back to the space of the living room—its high ceiling, pale, clinical walls and wide expanse of glass—the sound of her breathing rasping in her head.

She needed to clear her brain—to think—to plan. That was what she did best, what she was valued for. She wasn't just some pathetic creature at the mercy of her hormones. And this was just another problem needing a solution.

And, knowing all that, why did she want to throw

back her head and howl like a dog? she asked herself in bitter derision.

For a moment she stood, torn by indecision, then, snatching up her bag, Zanna left the apartment on the run, heading for the private underground car park. Although it was still early, the working day was beginning, and soon the inevitable barrage of phone calls would start too. The enquiries she would have to fend off. The questions she could not answer. The hammering at defences which were suddenly vulnerable.

And for a while she needed to distance herself. To regroup her personal resources.

She picked a route out of the city totally at random, or so she told herself. It was only when she was actually on the motorway that she realised, or admitted, where instinct was driving her.

But even so she didn't have to go through with it. She could still make the wise choice. Take the next exit— get out—get off. Go anywhere but there. She watched the road signs ripple past, each with its promise of a new destination, a new refuge. Watched and did nothing.

When the time came she eased across to the nearside lane as if she were an automaton. Within five minutes the tall hedges of the lanes had closed around her, pulling her inexorably into their depths, although she still wasn't sure what she was doing here or what she hoped to achieve by returning. She only knew that she had been drawn back as if by invisible cords, that no other choice had existed but to find Jake and—and then—what?

None of her training in negotiation or confrontation had prepared her for this kind of scenario. But she could at least talk to him, she amended lamely.

She was trembling as she drove past the village sign. She slowed when she reached the garage, but the doors were closed and padlocked and the place seemed deserted. Zanna bit her lip and drove on into the village.

She parked at the side of Church House, out of sight of the village green, and walked slowly up the path to the front door, trying to pretend she felt at ease when in reality she was shaking inside.

She rang the doorbell and waited, heart thudding, praying for some sign of movement inside the house, but there was only silence. As she went round to the back of the house she glimpsed a neatness and order between the parted curtains that spoke of emptiness and absence. Not just 'not at home' but 'gone away', she thought, her heart like a stone in her chest.

But what had made her think he'd be there? Had she really imagined she could simply step back into the enchantment and find him waiting, like the prince in a fairy tale, to kiss her and make her somehow whole again? She lashed herself with contempt. To make the nightmare go away? As if it had all meant something more—something finer than the usual sordid, casual one-night stand?

I didn't know I had such a talent for fantasy, she told herself angrily. Or such a capacity for self-deception.

She hammered on the back door, barking her knuckles, taking a kind of perverse pleasure in the discomfort of it. One glance through the kitchen window revealed the big pine table stripped and bare of any homely clutter.

The caretaker was no longer taking care, she thought, and realised for the first time how completely she'd relied on his being here for her, in this house which meant so much—how totally she'd needed to go into his arms and weep out her fear and confusion, to know the reality of his heart beating against hers.

And she wondered, not for the first time, what it had

been like for him to wake and find her gone, without a word. She wondered if he'd cared, if he'd asked at the Bull for any clues to 'Susie Smith' or tried to trace her in some other way.

Or if, more likely, he'd just accepted it for what it was—a passing fling, without strings or regrets, a few hours of total irresponsibility, now, at this distance, barely remembered.

Except by me, Zanna thought bleakly, and perhaps I should be thankful that pregnancy's been the only consequence of this incredible piece of folly.

She sat down limply on the stone step, leaning her back against the heavy timber. Life moved on, she thought, and it was unwise even to look back, let alone walk back into the past and hope to find it unchanged.

But, although she hadn't admitted it until this moment, she now realised that she had hoped and she had believed. And that made her present sense of desolation even more overwhelming. And more absurd.

Tears scalded like dancing fireflies behind her closed eyelids. His name burned on her aching throat.

'Where are you?' she whispered painfully into the stillness. 'Jake, come back—I need you. Forgive me for running away—and help me, please. Oh, please...'

She heard her words vanish into the unmoving silence and become swallowed up there. And after a while she got up slowly and stiffly from the step and went back to her car.

She got back to London in the early afternoon. She hadn't hurried the return journey, her mind circling wearily on her problems throughout the miles. Although she still hadn't come up with any real solution, she acknowledged unhappily as she fitted her key into its lock. And stopped, her senses alerted by the pungent odour of cigar smoke.

'Father?' she said uncertainly as she walked into the living room. 'What are you doing here?'

'Waiting for you.' The bulk of Sir Gerald's frame outlined against the window spoke of menace. 'You dirty little slut.'

Zanna's mouth was suddenly dry. 'I don't understand.'

'Neither did I—not until I went into the bathroom and found that obscene—thing.' His eyes were like stone. Opaque, cold. 'I had Ben Wickham with me. Tessa had told me about the vomiting. I was concerned, naturally. I wanted him to look you over.'

Zanna cursed Tessa under her breath. 'I asked her not to tell you. I said I didn't want the company doctor...'

'Thank God I have some employees who are loyal.' He drew a breath. 'I couldn't believe it when Ben told me what that paraphernalia was for—what it meant.'

Zanna lifted her chin. 'You have no right to come in here, either of you, and pry into my life. How did you get in anyway?'

'This apartment belongs to the company. I have keys to all Westcott property. And thank the Lord we did find out about you. The whole situation can be taken care of at once, without fuss or any scandal. Ben's assured me of that.'

Zanna was very still. 'What are you talking about?'

'He knows an excellent clinic, quick and discreet. He's making an appointment for you there right away.'

Zanna's head went back. 'You mean I'm to have an abortion?' Her mind was reeling. She seemed to be looking at her father across some vast chasm of space.

'Well, naturally,' he said impatiently.

She drew a swift breath. 'You haven't even asked who the father is. If we have our own plans...'

'I don't have to.' He drew heavily on the cigar. 'There's no ring on your finger or regular man in your life. I know that. You've behaved like a slut and a fool, but you don't have to live with the consequences—not these days.'

She stared at him. She said thickly, 'You're talking about your grandchild...'

'You think I'd actually welcome some bastard? That I'd let you humiliate me—Westcott Holdings—in front of the whole City?' His laugh was harshly derisive. 'See sense, girl. Remember who you are—what your purpose in life is.'

'Perhaps I don't see it as destroying unborn children.' She tried to speak calmly, evenly.

'Then you're worse than an idiot, and no daughter of mine.' Across the room, she felt the power of him—the anger like a tangible thing, reaching out to tear at her. 'Understand this, Zanna, there's no question of you keeping this child—becoming a—a single parent.' He spat the words at her. 'Do that and you lose everything— your job, your car and this flat. You're out on your ear and on your own, surviving on Social Security. See if the baby's father wants you then,' he added savagely.

'That's blackmail.'

'That's common sense,' Sir Gerald retorted implacably. 'You don't need to ruin your life, throw away your career because you've done a stupid thing.'

'I seem to have done a number of stupid things,' Zanna said tonelessly. 'But you and I would never agree on what they've been.'

Her father moved away from the window, and in spite of herself Zanna flinched as he came towards her. He stabbed out his cigar in a small porcelain dish, grinding the burning stub into the delicate glaze.

'I meant what I said,' he threw over his shoulder as he went past her to the door. 'I'm warning you, keep the appointment Ben's making for you, or you're finished.'

She heard the outer door slam and the tension went out of her. Knees buckling, she stumbled to the nearest sofa and sat down.

She stared around her.

My flat, she thought. The glittering prize I've worked myself into the ground for. The proof of my value and success. Or so I thought.

She looked at the gloss on the carefully chosen pieces of furniture, the unmarked pastel walls, the statements made by the few paintings and ceramics the designer had suggested, and wondered for the first time in her life what it all meant. How it could be that she'd made so little impression on her surroundings that they looked brand-new—untouched by human hand.

And inside her, also brand-new, was a tiny life, on which, for good or ill, she could be a major influence. And she knew that despite her father's threats her choice had already been made. There was no way she could ever have destroyed her child—Jake's child—the evidence that, just for once, during one reckless night in her sterile, work-orientated life, she had been human too.

You're finished. The brutal words seemed to echo in her mind. Slowly she shook her head, emptying them away.

No, she thought, with resolution. I'm just beginning.

CHAPTER SEVEN

NOT having a car placed a new value on your feet, Zanna thought wryly as she emerged from yet another employment agency.

Finding a bed-sitting room had been relatively easy, but so far, during the three weeks since her precipitate departure from Westcott Holdings, her job search had been totally fruitless.

Zanna had confidently believed that her track record would smooth her path into another executive position, but she'd been swiftly proved wrong.

Probably, she admitted, she had not really believed her father would go to the threatened lengths. But, arriving at the office the day after she had quietly but firmly told Dr Wickham that she would not be keeping the appointment he'd arranged for her to terminate her pregnancy, she had found her way barred by a clearly embarrassed security guard.

She'd been forced to wait in Reception until Tessa Lloyd, brimming with ill-concealed triumph, had arrived to conduct her to her office and stand over her while she cleared her desk. And before leaving she'd been required to hand back her car keys.

After that Zanna had seen no point in waiting for the humiliation of eviction from the flat, so she'd packed her clothes and her home computer and moved out to a hotel, using it as a base to start her hunt for a new home and employment.

Fortunately, shortage of money had not been an immediate problem, although she couldn't live indefinitely on her savings, which were ebbing away at frightening speed.

No, her main difficulty was that her name seemed to have become poison in the marketplace. Every job application she submitted ran into some kind of invisible barrier, and her total lack of references, added to brief, snide comments about her sudden departure in the financial pages of the daily Press, suggested she'd been guilty of some stunning misdemeanour. Fraud, at the very least, she'd realised with helpless horror. And she knew her father was at the back of it all. It was part of her on-going punishment for defying him. Although, from a practical point of view, he clearly didn't want Zanna taking her expertise to some rival company.

Candour about the real reason for her dismissal hadn't helped either. Companies were unlikely, she'd been told civilly but dismissively, to hire a young woman who would soon be asking them to pay for her maternity leave—especially when there was no guarantee that she'd return to work after the birth.

Gritting her teeth, Zanna had started applying for secretarial posts and making the weary rounds of the temping agencies. But many of them, including the one she'd just left, already had sufficient people on their books to supply current demand. Jobs weren't easy to come by, she was told regretfully. It was all part of the recession.

Now, pausing in the sunlit street while she flexed her aching toes in their smart court shoes, she pondered whether her volatile stomach was ready to tolerate some coffee. She had learned by bitter experience to start the day with a glass of mineral water and a dry biscuit, and to take things one step at a time thereafter.

But there weren't any coffee-shops in this particular street, she thought ruefully. It was all art galleries and antique shops, interspersed with the occasional designer

boutique. The kind of place she'd have found a happy
hunting ground in former days. Suppressing a sigh, she
decided to walk to Fortnum and Mason.

Waiting to cross the road, she found herself gazing
almost absently at a display of vibrant abstract art behind
an imposing stretch of plate glass. New since I was here
last, she thought, scrutinising the name emblazoned
across the immaculate dark green awning.

Lantrell Galleries, she repeated silently. Now, why did
that sound familiar? She'd reached the other pavement
before she remembered that, for some obscure reason, in
some other existence, she'd been invited to the opening.
She glanced irresolutely at her watch, then made up her
mind. As she was on the doorstep she might as well pay
them a belated visit.

She pushed open the heavy glass door and went in.
She was immediately aware of light and space and colour, of the subtle scent of polished wood and expensive
fabrics and a wide and shallow ramp leading in a gentle
semi-circle to an upper floor. The atmosphere was discreetly luxurious, she thought, glancing round her, and
totally inviting.

'Welcome to Lantrells.' The receptionist was the
epitome of blonde chic, but her smile was genuinely
warm as she handed Zanna a catalogue. 'Is this your first
visit to us? I'm afraid the current exhibition is nearly
over, and much of the work has been sold, but if you're
interested in any particular artist, our staff will be happy
to advise you.'

'Thank you.' Zanna returned the smile with a touch
of awkwardness, aware that she was there under false
pretences. 'I—I'd just like to browse.'

'Could I ask you to sign our visitors' register?' The
girl pushed across a smart leather-bound book, already

thick with names. 'Then we can keep you up to date
with our future exhibitions.'

Zanna took the pen and added her signature. Not that
she could make an offer for even a few inches of frame
in her present circumstances, she reflected as she turned
away.

I wish I knew more about painting, she thought as she
moved slowly from canvas to canvas. I wish I'd bought
pictures like this for the flat, instead of allowing the
decorator to choose for me. I wish... And there she
stopped, because this was a third wish and might just be
granted, and she didn't know what she would wish for.

Don't lie, she thought, staring up at a vast canvas of
overlapping circles and triangles in black and every con-
ceivable shade of red. You know exactly what you want.
That's why you went back to Emplesham to look for
him. You've known all the time—when you've allowed
yourself to think about it.

And even as she felt the hand, gentle on her shoulder,
and his voice say, very quietly, 'Susie,' all she could
think, absurdly, was, But I didn't make the wish—I
didn't say it. Then the circles and triangles were swirling
madly around her, drawing her forward and down into
some inner core of darkness.

'What wish?' said Jake.

She was lying on the downy comfort of a sofa in a
room that was clearly an office. She'd regained consciousness to find herself being carried up the ramp in
his arms, amid a buzz of consternation.

'What happened, Mr Lantrell? Did she just collapse?'

'Should we call a doctor, Mr Lantrell—an ambu-
lance?'

'No,' Zanna had roused herself to say, despite her dry
mouth and swimming head. 'No, I'll be fine.'

The blonde receptionist had brought her a glass of water. An older woman had dashed in with a tray of coffee.

Now, they were alone, and he was a few yards away, across the room from her, half-sitting on the edge of a vast desk. The dark elegance of his suit, the comparative sobriety of his trimmed hair made him seem alien, a stranger. As indeed he was, Zanna reminded herself as she struggled to sit up, hating the vulnerability of her supine position...

Not Jake Brown, in whose arms she'd learned the meaning of rapture, but someone quite different, and a thousand miles from the beguiling gipsy she'd run back to find.

Jake Lantrell, she thought. The owner of all this discreet opulence. A man of power. Someone she didn't know at all and couldn't afford to know.

She said, nervously pulling her skirt over her knees, 'I—I don't understand.'

'Before you passed out, you said something about making a wish.'

'Did I?' She tried to laugh, but the sound was high-pitched and unnatural. 'Put it down to the effect of shock on an overloaded nervous system.'

'Was it such a shock?'

'Oh, yes.' She moistened dry lips with the tip of her tongue. She thought, And it still is...

'After all,' she went on quickly, 'car mechanic into gallery owner is quite a metamorphosis.'

His mouth twisted in acknowledgment. 'All the same,' he said softly. 'I didn't think you'd swoon at my feet when I found you again.'

'You hardly found me,' Zanna objected feebly. 'I just—walked in from the street.'

'A lucky chance,' he agreed. 'But it doesn't alter the

fact that I've been searching for you. Or did you think I'd just let you vanish like that?'

She was very still suddenly. She said, 'I hoped you'd understand my wishes—and respect them.'

He shook his head. 'Unfortunately, I'm not a great respecter of wishes that don't coincide with my own.' There was a pause. 'You didn't suspect anything when I sent you the invitation to the opening?'

'No, how could I?' Zanna looked down at her clasped hands. 'After all, it wasn't addressed to Susie Smith.'

His smile reached out to her. The dark eyes lingered on her face, her mouth, then moved down to her breasts. 'Perhaps it should have been. But I wanted us to start again, without pretence this time.'

She felt her heart begin to thud, half in trepidation, half in nervous excitement. Be careful, she warned herself silently. The dark path of his attraction was not something she dared to tread again.

'When did you find out—who I really was?'

'It didn't take long to establish.' His expression was enigmatic.

'No, probably not.' She paused. 'But was it really worth the trouble—for such a brief encounter?'

'I think so. After all, you and I have a lot of unfinished business, Susie.'

She lifted her head, tried to speak crisply. 'If you're so well-informed, you should know I'm always called Zanna.'

He lifted a negligent shoulder. 'I don't regard it as an improvement.'

'You have one hell of a nerve.'

'You don't get far in this life without it. And you've shown a fair bit yourself, leaving the security blanket of Daddy's company,' he added smoothly. 'How are you finding the real world?'

He was altogether too well-informed, damn him.
Zanna drew a breath, wondering exactly how deeply his
researches had probed. Not, she hoped, to the antenatal
unit of a famous teaching hospital. 'Interesting,' she returned crisply.

'Found another job yet?'

Zanna hesitated, smarting. 'I'm waiting for the right
opportunity,' she countered.

'In other words, no.' His mouth twisted. 'Being refused anything must be a new experience for you, Susie.'

'One of many,' she said airily. 'I know about gas me-
ters now, and public transport, as well as sharing a bathroom and a thousand things to do with baked beans.'

'Why did you leave Westcott Holdings?'

It wasn't the question she was expecting—if there
could be such a thing from Jake, she thought bitterly.

'A—difference of opinion,' she temporised.

'With your father?'

'Who else?' She made herself smile. 'Contrary to rumour, I did not transfer the petty cash to a numbered
Swiss bank account.'

The dark brows rose. 'I'm glad to hear it, although
that particular rumour had passed me by.'

Her hands clenched together in her lap. 'So, what have
you heard?' She tried to sound amused, but every muscle
was tense.

'That there's been a parting of the ways, personally
as well as professionally. I went round to the place
where you used to live and the security man told me
you'd left.'

And I, she thought, went round to the place where
you used to live and found it empty too. But that's something else I intend to keep secret.

She said coolly, 'I really can't understand why you
should bother.'

'I told you—we have unfinished business.'

She shook her head. 'On the contrary. We met, we spent some time together and we parted.' She looked down at her clenched hands. 'That's how I want it. Coming here today was just—an unfortunate coincidence.'

'Is that a fact? Now I wouldn't have said you were a girl for one-night stands, Susie.'

'But then, in spite of all your research, you still don't know a great deal about me,' Zanna parried.

His mouth quirked. 'I'd have said we were intimately acquainted,' he drawled.

She felt his gaze touch her like the caress of a hand, and shivered inwardly as she remembered...

She bit her lip, forcing herself back to the present, and reality.

'I'm afraid I find this a tasteless conversation. You're quite right, of course. I don't usually behave as I did that night, and I don't want to be reminded of it—or to repeat it either.'

'That,' he said, 'was not what I was suggesting.' He swung himself off the desk and walked forward. He sat down beside her and took her chin in his hand, tilting her face towards him in spite of her immediate and instinctive resistance.

'You've been having a bad time,' he said abruptly. 'You've lost weight and you've got enormous shadows under your eyes.'

'Aren't you the flatterer,' she managed from a dry throat. His actual touch had set her every pulse hammering, she realised with vexation.

'I'm stating a fact.' He released her. 'Have dinner with me tonight.'

It was more a command than a request, and Zanna

stiffened. This was a situation she needed to avoid at all costs, she thought, swallowing.

'No,' she said. 'Thank you.'

'Is there something wrong with my table manners?'

'Don't get paranoid,' she advised crisply. 'I'm busy, that's all.'

'Tomorrow night?'

'Not then either.'

He tutted. 'Playing hard to get, Susie?'

'Not before time, perhaps,' she said with cool irony. She paused. 'I'm sure you've heard the saying about ships that pass in the night. I'd like to leave it like that.'

He shook his head. The dark eyes held hers almost mesmerically. 'We didn't pass, Susie. We collided.'

She shrugged. 'Well, everyone's entitled to one major error. I'll consider that mine. But I don't intend to compound the fault.' She transferred her gaze back to her lap. 'Tell me something. Why were you in Emplesham?'

'Looking after a house.'

Her brows snapped together. 'Oh, please,' she said sarcastically. 'You have all this—' she gestured around her '—and fill in as a caretaker at weekends? Is that what you're saying?'

'No, that's what you're saying. I keep an eye on Church House for my father.'

'But you said it belonged to a Mr Gordon.'

He nodded laconically. 'Gordon Lantrell.'

'So you were even fooling me about that,' she said bitterly.

'You were the one who wanted to play games,' he said. 'I just invented a few of my own rules.'

'Please don't remind me,' she flung back at him. 'Your car mechanic act was wonderfully convincing too.'

'Thank you,' he returned politely. 'But it wasn't totally make-believe. Steve who owns the garage is semi-retired now, and he lets me borrow it when it's free. Naturally I pay for the electricity.'

'Oh, naturally,' she echoed derisively. 'A paragon of probity.'

'And working on classic cars like the Jag has always been a passion of mine,' Jake went on, without apparently noticing her interjection. 'You could say it's my favourite form of relaxation.' He paused. 'Or one of them, at least.'

He was far too close to her, the amusement dancing in his eyes and curving his firm mouth an all too potent force. Zanna got to her feet, clumsy in her haste.

'Careful.' He stood up too, with a steadying hand under her elbow. 'I don't want you fainting again.'

'That isn't likely,' Zanna said tartly, wrenching herself free. 'I don't make a habit of it. It—it must have been the heat.'

'I hope not. The temperature in the gallery is carefully controlled.' He paused. 'A quality you appear to share.'

'Better late than never.' She made herself meet his gaze. 'That girl that night—in the house at Emplesham—she never existed. You must understand that. Accept it. I—I don't really know what happened.'

'Don't you?' His tone was almost reflective. 'At a guess, I'd say that life happened to you, Susie.'

'And please stop calling me that.' She punched her fist into the palm of her other hand in frustration. 'There is no "Susie". There never was.'

'I'm sorry to hear that. I shall miss her.' Another deliberate pause. 'Suzannah.'

'I never use that name either.'

'May I know why?'

'My mother's name was Susan. After she died my father found it too painful a reminder, so I became

Zanna.' And why, she asked herself helplessly, have I told him all that?

'I'm sure you did,' he said quietly. 'Except for a few brief hours which you're now doing your damnedest to deny.'

'I have my reasons,' she said shortly. 'I'm sure I don't need to spell them out.'

'On the contrary,' Jake drawled. 'We might both find it—instructive. But I'll let you off, Ms Westcott, as we're being formal, on one condition.'

'Which is?' Zanna picked up her bag, prepared for flight.

'What I asked at the beginning of this somewhat tortuous interview. I want you to tell me what you were wishing for.'

'Easily done,' she said tautly. 'I was wishing that you and I had never met.'

There was a brief silence, then, 'How sad,' he said lightly, 'when we share such beautiful memories. And here's another for the collection.'

His hands descended on her shoulders, pulling her towards him, and his mouth covered hers in a swift, angry possession which left her breathless. It was a fierce ravishment, over as soon as it had begun, which left her treacherous, reeling senses crying out for more. She wanted to feel the warmth of his body against hers, the strength of his arms holding her, comforting her. And instead she was left with—nothing.

She stepped back, resisting the temptation to put a hand to her throbbing lips. Her words, it seemed, had caught him on the raw.

'Game over.' She was annoyed to hear the slight tremor in her voice. 'Goodbye, Mr Lantrell.'

His smile had all the charm in the world. 'Good riddance, Ms Westcott.'

He did not touch her again, but somehow she found herself ushered out, found herself negotiating the ramp to the ground floor, aware of the sidelong glances of the staff.

And the sound of his door, closing behind her, echoed in her brain with a curious finality all the way to the street.

The park was busy. As well as tourists, office and shop workers had brought their lunches into one of London's great open spaces and were picnicking on the grass, enjoying the warmth of the sun. And there were families too, playing ball and feeding crusts of bread to the ducks and swans on the lake.

Zanna, huddled in solitary state on a bench near the sparkling water, watched them with unseeing eyes. In spite of the heat, she felt deathly cold.

She was still trying to come to terms with the events of the past hour, to accept that Jake had been here in London, looking for her, at the same time as she'd been in Emplesham, trying to find him. Except it wasn't like that, she reminded herself fiercely.

Because Jake Brown, who'd teased her, infuriated her, warmed her and carried her away on a tide of undreamed-of passion, had never existed.

And in his place was a man more of an enigma than his sham counterpart had ever been.

Not that there was any real mystery about why he'd tried to find her, she acknowledged bitterly. She could guess the nature of their 'unfinished business' all too easily, in spite of his denial. He'd intended their relationship to resume where it had left off—in bed. He'd been intrigued by her summary departure sufficiently to pursue her, to discover her real identity—something he'd achieved without too many problems.

But thank God his investigations hadn't gone any deeper, she thought, laying a protective hand on her abdomen. At least he didn't know about the baby.

She hadn't been sure, even when she went back to Emplesham to find him, whether she would actually tell Jake Brown she was going to have his child. She knew without any doubt at all that she would keep it a secret from Jake Lantrell.

Even if he didn't react like that other man of power, her father, and suggest she had an abortion, he would insist on offering her money for the baby's upkeep, and that would entail a measure of control. Even worse, he might feel sorry for her, she thought, wincing as pain slashed through her.

Well, she wanted neither his pity, his money, nor his involvement in her life. And she could do without them. She could cope.

It would probably mean leaving London, she acknowledged. She might also have to change her name, because she wasn't convinced he wouldn't come after her again. Jake Lantrell was hardly a man to take no for an answer, or to relish such a cavalier dismissal as she'd tried to inflict.

She would have to run, she told herself, and she would have to hide. And there was no more time to waste.

Shivering, she reached for her bag, then paused, transfixed, as she watched the group coming towards her. It was another family party, the man tall and dark, the woman shorter, slighter, fairer, and their child, just emerging from babyhood, toddling between them, clasping a hand of each. As they walked along the parents were swinging him gently into the air while he squealed with delight, demanding to be swung again as soon as his feet touched the ground.

Zanna saw the look they exchanged over the laughing

child's head, proud, tender, adoring, and felt her throat tighten in response.

That, she thought, was how it should be. How, surely, it *must* be, rather than the lonely road she had chosen.

She knew now, clearly and without equivocation, why she'd tried so desperately to find Jake. Because for a few short hours she'd encountered her man, the other half of herself—or so she'd believed.

Only now, she thought, he's gone for ever. And she saw the shimmering water in front of her dissolve and blur as her eyes filled with tears she dared not shed.

CHAPTER EIGHT

ZANNA cut open the pack of moist pink ham and regarded it with distaste. Salad, she thought with a sigh, and new potatoes to prettify it, and plenty of pickle to mask its total lack of flavour. Or, better still, why didn't she forget the ham and simply empty the pickle jar?

Zanna Westcott, she reproached herself, do you want this child to be born with a permanently sour expression?

Certainly since she'd been pregnant her appetite for sharp and spicy foods had increased enormously. But this evening, she didn't have much of an appetite at all.

You have to eat, she told herself firmly. You've made decisions. You have plans. You need to keep your strength up.

On leaving the park, she'd caught one of the open-top tour buses and spent the afternoon riding round and round while she recovered her composure, looking at a London she'd barely known up to now. It was time she saw the sights and learned to appreciate some of its history and grandeur, she'd thought wryly, especially as she would be leaving very soon.

She'd decided to move to one of the big Northern cities—Manchester, perhaps, or Leeds. It would be easier to start again—make a new life in a place where she was completely unknown. It would be an adventure, she thought with determination.

She wondered what her chances were of reclaiming some of the rent she'd paid in advance from the landlord, and concluded ruefully that they were probably slim. Her room was clean, and decently furnished, but that was as far as his philanthropy went. However, she'd written to him, to hand in her notice, leaving her letter in his post box downstairs.

She considered her dwindling financial resources and grimaced. She'd travel by coach, because it was cheaper than the train, find the cheapest possible digs and sign on with every employment agency she could find. She'd take any job she was offered and save every penny she could towards a decent flat for when the baby was born. And when she couldn't work any longer she'd claim maternity benefit. It was all perfectly straightforward, she told herself resolutely.

And Jake Lantrell could spend as much time as he liked searching London for her. Until, of course, he got fed up and decided to call off his dogs.

'Another problem solved,' she said under her breath as she filled a saucepan with water for the potatoes and set it to boil on her tiny gas stove.

The knock at her door surprised her. It must be the landlord coming to check she hadn't done a flit with everything she could carry, she decided grimly as she went to answer it.

She said coolly, 'I didn't expect such an immediate reaction...' and stopped dead, gasping, as she saw who was waiting outside.

'I hope you're not going to faint again.' Jake held up a carrier bag and a wrapped bottle of wine. 'As you see, my hands are full this time, and I won't be able to catch you.'

She said grittily, 'What the hell are you doing here?'

'I asked you to have dinner with me. You refused, so I'm here to have dinner with you. I've even brought the food, which I reckon makes me the perfect guest.'

'I'm sure you think you're very amusing.' Her face

was stony. 'But I regard this as harassment, and I want
you to leave. Now.'

Jake shook his head sadly. 'Hospitality isn't what it
was.'

'I think,' she said, 'that you're supposed to wait till
it's offered.'

'Maybe,' he agreed. 'But I had the feeling it might be
a long wait.'

'Until hell freezes over,' Zanna corroborated. She
wished he would go, and quickly. Because the smell
from the carrier bag was utterly delectable. Chinese, she
thought hungrily, her mouth beginning to water.

'Are you sure I can't persuade you to dine with me?'
He looked past her to the small table, where that damned
ham was already pessimistically curling at the corners.
'Although what you're having looks delicious, of
course,' he added smoothly.

'Are you sure you won't just leave the food and go?'
she retorted.

'No way, Susie.' His grin was appreciative. 'This is a
take-away special dinner for two. You have to learn to
share.'

She hesitated. 'I thought I'd made it clear I didn't
want to see you again.'

'You made it crystal-clear that you didn't want to pick
up where we left off,' he said crisply. 'But that doesn't
mean we can't be friends. Let's say that we didn't part
on the best of terms this morning, and I'd like to make
amends.'

She gave him a troubled look. 'This is not a good
idea.'

'Neither is eating alone in this grisly hole.' Jake gave
his surroundings a scathing look. 'Is this the best you
could do?'

She shrugged. 'You tell me,' she countered. 'You

seem to be the self-appointed expert on my affairs. And you should see some of the places I turned down.'

'No thanks. It might put me off my food. Speaking of which…' Jake held up the carrier bag, sending more delicious scents wafting towards her. 'Are you going to let me in, or is all this wonderful crispy duck and pork and prawn and black bean sauce just going to waste?'

She stood aside grudgingly. 'Well—OK.'

'There's my gracious hostess.' He began to unpack foil cartons onto the table. 'Does this establishment run to two plates? I've brought chopsticks. And this.' He handed her a short length of rope, tied in a coil.

'What's this for?' Zanna looked at it, mystified.

'I thought you might want the additional assurance of tying my hands behind my back,' he said. 'Of course, you'd have to feed me.'

Her lips curved into a reluctant smile. 'Don't be a fool. Besides, what makes you think I wouldn't tie you up and eat the lot in front of you?'

'Zanna might,' he said. 'But Susie? Never.'

'I wish you'd stop this,' she protested. 'You make me feel like a split personality.'

'I'm not sure that's so wide of the mark.' His mouth twisted wryly as he uncorked the wine. 'Glasses?'

'No wine for me, thanks.' She spoke without thinking as she reached into the cupboard for just one glass.

His brows lifted. 'Have you signed the pledge?'

She flushed defensively. 'Of course not. I just feel it might be—wiser to keep my wits about me, that's all.'

'And I give you my word that's not a problem.' His glance flicked derisively sideways to the narrow single bed with its candlewick spread. 'I want us to be friends. Nothing more.' He held up the bottle. 'Now get yourself a glass and we'll drink a toast to being good companions.'

Reluctantly, she complied. To tell him she'd given up alcohol on health grounds might be a damaging admission under the circumstances, she realised. Jake wasn't stupid. He'd be as capable of putting two and two together as the next man.

She forced a smile. 'Not crystal, I'm afraid.' And she would allow herself just a few sips, she thought.

'Nor a particularly good year, I suspect,' he returned drily. 'The off-licence round the corner seems to specialise in lager.' He lifted his glass. 'To friendship, Suzannah.'

'To friendship,' she echoed obediently, adding silently, *however short-lived*.

She wished she could trust him—but it was impossible. He'd already proved that he could be just as manipulative and determined as her father, and she was never going to allow anyone into a position of such control again.

The food tasted as good as it had smelt. Strange how ravenous you were when offered exactly what you wanted, Zanna thought dreamily as she finished off the crispy duck.

'That's better.' Jake said approvingly. 'A couple of weeks' cossetting and you should be back to your normal weight.'

And surpassing it, Zanna thought ruefully. Her obstetrician had told her that a slight weight loss was quite common in the early part of pregnancy, but that she'd soon make up for it.

Her brows lifted questioningly. 'Cossetting?'

'That's clearly what you need. Unless I miss my guess, there hasn't been too much of it in your life.'

'Please don't feel sorry for me,' Zanna said curtly, putting down her chopsticks. 'By most people's standards I've had a charmed existence.'

He sighed. 'Suzannah, I'm trying to get to know you. But you don't make it particularly easy.'

She shrugged. 'Perhaps I value my privacy.' She gave him a level look. 'I seem to have very little of it.'

'You're angry because I tracked you down?'

'More baffled by your persistence.'

'I do have my reasons.'

She was sure he did. She looked at him across the table, at the watchful eyes, the faint smile playing about his mouth. She remembered the taste of his mouth, the stroke of his hands on her naked flesh, and felt her body clench in sudden, shocking need. As she sought to control the flurry in her breathing she wondered what he remembered.

'And one day you'll tell me what they are?' She kept her voice calm.

He nodded. 'One day.'

This year, she thought, next year, some time, *never*.

She rose, collected the plates together and carried them to the sink. 'Would you like coffee?' She made the offer polite but cool.

'I'd prefer some real conversation.' There was a certain grimness in his tone as he filled the kettle and set it to boil.

'Who gets to choose the subject?'

'Talk about whatever you want.'

'Very well.' She spooned coffee into the cafetière. 'Tell me about Lantrell's. I believe you have galleries all over the world?'

'That's the ultimate aim. The first one was opened by my great-grandfather in New York. He'd made a lot of money from oil, but art was his passion. Discovering new talent and providing it with a showcase was the joy of his life. It all grew from there.'

'He was American, then?'

'Very much so. You sound surprised.'

'A little.' She paused. 'You don't have an accent.'

'We're quite a cosmopolitan family. My grandmother was French and my mother English. I went to school here, and to university.'

'Oh,' she said. 'I suppose that's why your father bought the house in Emplesham—for vacations and so on?'

'That was one of the reasons, certainly.'

'But you've only just opened in London? Isn't that rather strange?'

He shrugged. 'My predecessors had other priorities. But it was always going to happen eventually.' He paused. 'It was a pity you missed the opening.'

'I'm sure it was a very glamorous occasion. I like the lay-out. There's a great sense of space and peace.'

'That's down to my stepmother,' he said. 'She insists that the eye has to be given time to see and appreciate properly.'

'I'm sure she's right.' She hesitated. 'You said your stepmother…?'

He nodded. 'My own mother died when I was small.'

'I'm sorry,' she said stiltedly. 'I—I know what that's like. Do you remember her?'

'Yes, very well.'

'You're—fortunate in that respect. I was only a baby.' She swallowed. 'Do you get on with your stepmother?'

'Yes. She's a terrific woman and a great lady. She's made my father very happy.'

She said slowly, 'Perhaps my father should have married again. It can't have been easy for him—being alone.'

'Loneliness can be damaging,' he agreed quietly.

Zanna, adding boiling water to the cafetière, looked at him sharply. 'My father,' she said with emphasis, 'is one of the most successful businessmen in the country. Hardly damaged goods.'

He said unsmilingly, 'I stand corrected. I also wonder if he'd be so ready to leap to your defence.'

'That,' she said, 'is none of your business.'

'What was the quarrel about, Susie?'

'You mean your tracker dog doesn't go in for industrial espionage too?' She could have bitten her tongue out. The last thing she wanted was for Jake or anyone to start probing around Westcott Holdings. All it would take would be an indiscreet comment from Megan, say, about her mystery illness, and her secret would be out. And she wasn't prepared to risk that.

'Almost certainly,' Jake returned equably. 'But I'd rather hear it from you.'

'And I'd rather not discuss it,' she said crisply. 'Stalemate.'

'It's not just idle curiosity. I'd like to help, Susie. That's what friends are for, in case you didn't know.'

'And what is that supposed to mean?'

He shrugged. 'Merely that you must be feeling fairly isolated at the moment.'

'And along you come like Sir Lancelot to rescue me, I suppose?' She poured the coffee clumsily, hands shaking, spilling some into the saucers. 'Oh, damnation.'

'Let me do it.'

'I think you've done enough already.' She took a deep, steadying breath. 'I'd like you to drink your coffee and leave, please. You have a white horse to return to its stable.'

There was a silence. Jake said quietly, 'I really seem to have screwed up.'

'You said it.' She drank some coffee. It was scalding and oddly bitter, and she put the cup down again. 'I'm grateful for the meal. It was—wonderful. But that's as far as it goes. Save your compassion for a worthier cause.'

'I'm not being compassionate, Goddamn it.' There was a note of steel under the even voice. 'I want to be your friend, Suzannah.'

'We had sex once.' She put a hand on the back of the chair, gripped it till her knuckles turned white. 'That does not put me on your charity list. If I need a bloody Samaritan, the number's in the book.'

Jake threw back his head. The dark eyes were as cold as obsidian. He said, 'You win, Zanna.' There was an edge of contempt in his use of her name. 'I shan't try again.'

'That,' she said, 'is all I wanted to hear.'

They stood facing each other across the table. It was a cheap, narrow thing. All she had to do was reach out a hand and she could touch him. And, oh, dear God, how badly she wanted to touch him.

Ever since he'd entered the room she'd wanted him to come to her, to take her in his arms and assuage the shock, and fear and loneliness of the past weeks with his body. She'd needed to eclipse the confines of this room, the cramped, uncomfortable bed, with the generosity of her own giving. She longed to take him into her and hold him there through an eternity of pleasure.

I don't want you just as a friend, she screamed silently at him. I want you as my lover too. I want your passion as well as your kindness, and if I can't have that I'd rather have nothing. Nothing at all. How can you not see that? How can you not know?

And how strange, how awful, and how ironic that she should only be fully aware of this now—at this moment when she was sending him away for ever.

She watched him turn away, almost wearily. The door closed behind him and she could hear the sound of his footsteps receding down the uncarpeted stairway. She listened for the sound of the outer door but there was silence, enveloping the room like some cold, stifling miasma.

She released the back of the chair and started gently to rub her aching hand. The coil of rope was lying forgotten at her feet and she bent to retrieve it.

You win, Zanna. The words seemed to ring in her head, to claw at her brain.

She said shakily, 'Some victory,' and felt the first, helpless scald of tears rise in her throat and spill from her burning eyes.

'Miss Westcott.' The thump on the door came from one of her neighbours. 'Telephone for you.'

Zanna sat up groggily. After Jake's departure she had simply collapsed onto the bed and wept herself to sleep, waking in the small hours, cramped and cold. She'd undressed and crept under the blankets, lying still, staring blankly into the unmoving darkness. When sleep had finally returned, it had been frugal and restless, invaded by vague, disturbing dreams. Now, she realised with shock, it was almost midday, yet she still felt as if she hadn't closed her eyes all night. She stumbled out of bed, reaching for a robe, wondering who could be calling her.

She picked up the receiver, half in hope, half in dread. 'Zanna Westcott speaking.'

'Good morning.' A woman's voice. 'This is Diana Malan of First Appointment. You came to see us yesterday about temporary work.'

'Yes, I did.' Zanna shook the cobwebs from her brain and gathered her resources. 'The problem is, I've decided I'd rather work outside London.'

'Well, there's no real difficulty there.' Diana Malan

sounded amused. 'On the contrary. Do you have a current passport?'

'Why, yes.' Zanna frowned. 'Are you offering me a job abroad somewhere?'

'That's the plan,' the other woman said cheerfully. 'Could you call at the office this afternoon to discuss it, please? Shall we say three o'clock?'

Zanna assured her that would be ideal and put down the phone, her heart thudding.

Leaving the country, she thought, could be the answer to all her problems. The greater distance she could put between Jake and herself the better. Out of sight, out of mind. And, with luck, it would work both ways. He would write her off as the one that got away and she'd be able to erase him completely from her heart and brain.

At this time of day there was less pressure for occupation of the bathroom on her floor, so Zanna was able to enjoy a leisurely bath and wash her hair. She ironed a navy silk blouse to match her slim-fitting skirt, topping it with a neat scarlet blazer and completing her outfit with navy stockings and pumps. She looked reasonably smart, and businesslike at the same time, she thought, reviewing herself as best she could in the inadequate mirror.

She was marginally daunted when she realised that First Appointment had been her last port of call the previous morning, and was situated altogether too near the Lantrell Gallery for comfort. But Jake's office was at the rear of the building, she reminded herself. And, anyway, he'd be unlikely to be looking out for her.

Nevertheless, it was a relief to find herself, unaccosted, in Diana Malan's office, drinking coffee.

'On the form you completed for us, you stated that you spoke French.' Mrs Malan, small and chic in a black and white print dress and enormous pearl earrings, pressed one of the keys on her computer to call up the relevant information.

Zanna nodded. 'It was one of my ''A'' level subjects. I found it useful in my previous work, as we had a number of contacts in Europe.'

'You also say you have no commitments, so you could start at once?'

'Yes. I didn't expect you to offer me anything so soon.'

'Well, this is a new client, a recommendation from one of our regulars. She's an Englishwoman, living in the South of France, who requires a French-speaking secretary to replace her permanent girl.' Mrs Malan frowned at the screen. 'Apparently she's taking leave of absence to nurse her mother after a major operation.'

'So I'd be needed for—how long?' Zanna suppressed her growing excitement.

The other woman pursed her lips. 'At least six weeks—possibly two months.' She smiled at Zanna. 'I can't say your duties sound particularly onerous. Madame Cordet entertains for her husband, who's a businessman of some kind, so you'll be involved in a fair bit of social correspondence. And she's writing a book—some kind of history about the region.' She winked at Zanna. 'Heaven knows if it will ever be published, but that's not our problem.'

She turned back to the screen. 'Their house is in the hills behind Cannes, and there's a tennis court and a swimming pool—so go equipped. Your return air fare will be paid, and you'll be met at the airport by the chauffeur.'

'It sounds too good to be true.' Zanna shook her head in bewilderment.

'Maybe, but in my experience most Edens come complete with serpent.' Mrs Malan sounded philosophical.

'Maybe she's got a temper? Perhaps he's a groper? Whatever, it's temporary, and she's offering top rates. Can I notify her to expect you in three days' time?'

Zanna thought quickly. She could afford to store the personal items she wouldn't want to take with her. Then, when she came back, she could revert to Plan A and move north. In two months' time, of course, her pregnancy would be beginning to show. And it would be hot in France. Maybe she should dip into her depleted savings for some loose cool tops.

She smiled at Mrs Malan. 'I'll be ready,' she said. 'In fact, I can't wait.'

It was a scramble, but exactly three days later she was sitting in the plane, catching her first excited glimpse of the Mediterranean as they descended into Nice airport.

Don't be an idiot, she reproved herself, this is work not a holiday—although there'd been few enough of those since she'd started work. As a senior at school she'd been to France and Germany on visits to carefully selected families, usually business contacts of her father with daughters of a suitable age, but Sir Gerald had always regarded holidays as a disruption to the making of money. He personally wasn't interested in foreign travel, unless there was some deal involved, and he'd expected Zanna to take the same attitude.

Now she felt, absurdly, as if she'd been let out of jail.

She'd packed carefully, choosing simple skirts, trousers and a variety of tops, as well as several of her prettier formal dresses and some sportswear. It wasn't a huge selection, but she was there as a secretary, not a clothes-horse, she told herself with an inward shrug. And, if necessity arose, she could always make some judicious additions to her wardrobe from her salary, although she wanted to save as much of it as possible.

Meanwhile she prayed that Madame Cordet would be as charming as Mrs Malan said she sounded, and that her husband would keep his hands to himself. If so, it should all be plain sailing.

The written instructions from Mrs Malan told her to report at once to the airport enquiry desk after the immigration and customs formalities were complete.

Which couldn't happen too soon, she thought, fanning herself with her broad-brimmed straw hat.

'*Mademoiselle?*' The girl at the enquiry desk gave her a swift professional smile.

'I am to be met.' Zanna tried out her French. 'By the chauffeur of a Madame Cordet. Do you know if he has arrived?'

'*Bien sûr, mademoiselle.*' The girl looked past her, her smile widening. '*Monsieur* has been waiting for you,' she added almost reverently.

Which was an odd way to refer to a chauffeur, Zanna had time to think, before her case was taken from her hand.

She turned swiftly, the breath catching in her throat as she looked up at the new arrival.

'Hello, Zanna.' Jake's smile was cool and impersonal. 'Welcome to France.' And he bent to kiss her, lightly and formally, on each cheek.

CHAPTER NINE

'YOU.' Zanna could feel the colour draining out of her face as she looked up at him. She took an instinctive step backwards. 'What are you doing here?'

He looked faintly amused. 'Isn't it obvious? I'm meeting the plane.'

'But you were in London.' She was almost wringing her hands.

'I flew down yesterday. Our gallery in Nice had a slight problem that needed my attention.' He turned and started for the exit, carrying her case. She flew after him.

'Hold it right there,' she commanded raggedly. 'How did you know I'd be here? Did Madame Cordet tell you?'

He said slowly, 'Not exactly.'

Zanna threw back her head. 'Oh,' she said. 'I get it. This is a set-up!' Her breasts rose and fell under the force of her angry breathing. 'There is no job. There probably isn't a Madame Cordet either.'

Her voice had risen and people were turning their heads to stare curiously. The glances of the women were frankly appraising. In elegant cream trousers and a dark blue silk shirt, Jake looked toe-curlingly attractive, and this fuelled her resentment.

He said quietly, 'There certainly is. I've known her for fifteen years. And it might be better if we continued this discussion in the car.'

'Like hell it would,' Zanna flung at him. 'I'm going nowhere with you.'

'Well, you can't stay here. You're causing an obstruction.'

'You actually think this is funny, don't you?' she said unevenly. She held out an imperative hand. 'Well, laugh at this, Mr Brown—or Mr Lantrell—or whatever identity you're assuming today. I'm taking my case and flying straight back to England.'

'I'm afraid you'll find the return flight is fully booked.'

'Then I'll wait until there's a seat available.'

'And where do you plan to stay in the meantime?' He sounded politely interested.

She hesitated. 'There'll be hotels—*pensions*.'

'It's the height of the season and Nice is bursting at the seams.' He hadn't relinquished his hold on her case, she realised, seething. 'And can you really afford Côte d'Azur prices?'

'That,' she said curtly, 'is my problem.'

'No.' He wasn't smiling now. 'It's mine. Because you're quite correct. I did set this up.'

She said huskily, 'You had no right—no right at all.'

'I also had no choice.' His mouth twisted. 'I didn't think you'd accept a simple invitation to accompany me to the South of France.'

'Damned right I wouldn't.' Her mouth was dry and her heart was thudding against her ribs. 'I thought I'd made it clear that it was all over between us—over and done with.'

'You did, and I accept that.' His dark eyes gravely studied her flushed face. 'This isn't the time or the place to talk about this, but I want you to know that I deeply regret that night in Emplesham. It should never have happened. And I haven't got you here for a rerun, whatever you may be thinking.'

'You wouldn't like to know what I'm thinking.

Zanna lifted her chin. 'So why am I here? For my health?'

'Something like that,' he said calmly. 'I mentioned that you needed cossetting. I also know you need work. I thought bringing you down here would kill two birds with one stone.'

'You mean there really is a job with Madame Cordet?' Her mind was reeling. She could think of nothing but the words of regret he'd spoken a moment ago. Words she should have wanted to hear, because they set her free. Words that had hurt so much she could have cried aloud from the pain.

'Not with Sylvie, I'm afraid. She's your employer's housekeeper, and married to the chauffeur who's waiting for us outside.' His smile was tight. 'You see how pure my motives are? I've even brought along a chaperon.'

'Please don't expect me to be grateful. Or to take up your kind offer of employment. I don't want or need your charity.' Again she held out her hand. 'Now will you give me my case?'

He shook his head. 'I don't think I can do that. The earliest flight you can hope for is tomorrow, and I'm not leaving you stranded in Nice for twenty-four hours or more. Don't burden me with that on my conscience, along with all the rest.'

She said stonily, 'Then you shouldn't have—lured me down here under false pretences.'

'That's not strictly true. The job exists, so why not give it a chance? Let me take you up to Les Étoiles to meet your new boss. At least it'll mean you have a roof over your head tonight. If you still want to leave after that, I'll make sure you're on the first available plane back to the UK. Is it a deal?'

'I suppose so,' Zanna conceded reluctantly. If she was honest, the thought of tramping the streets of Nice with a heavy case, looking for cheap accommodation, appalled her.

'But there's one thing.' She halted him again. 'If I'm not working for Madame Cordet, then who's actually employing me?'

He said curtly, 'My stepmother,' and walked ahead of her out into the sunshine.

The car had air-conditioning, but Zanna was fully aware of the intensity of the heat baking against its panels just the same. Or was it simply the effect of her own anger and misery, fermenting in a confined space?

She sat rigidly beside Jake, staring unseeingly at the landscape outside the tinted windows. She knew that Maurice, the driver, had deliberately taken a route that would show her all the beauties of the coastline between Nice and Cannes, and Jake, too, had been quick to point out sights of interest when they reached the famous resort, but she felt totally remote. Like a fly, she thought, trapped in amber.

She still couldn't believe how gullible she'd been, believing that a job like this could simply fall into her lap. But then she'd wanted to believe that her luck had changed, that things were going her way, she thought unhappily.

She should have known that she wouldn't escape from him that easily.

Now, for reasons she still couldn't understand, she was travelling beside him to heaven knew where. The beautiful sea-front of Cannes, with its clustering yachts and chic restaurants, was far behind them now. They'd been climbing steadily into the hills for what seemed like hours.

But perhaps that was her imagination, heightened by the tension of Jake's proximity. His thigh was only inches away from her own on the luxurious leather seat. The sleeves of his shirt were casually rolled back and she could see the faint dusting of dark hair on his tanned skin. She was piercingly, hungrily aware of the clean, male scent of him.

There wasn't, she thought, an inch of him that she hadn't explored with her hands and mouth. Yet here they sat like strangers.

The silence was not one of intimacy, but she needed to break it anyway.

'How did you know I could be contacted through First Appointment?' she asked.

'I didn't, but it seemed logical,' he returned. 'You had to have some reason for being in that particular street.'

She said bitterly, 'I shall have a few things to say to Diana Malan when I get back.'

'You mustn't blame her. She was just doing her job.'

'And if I hadn't been able to speak French, or if my passport had been out of date—what then?' she challenged.

He shrugged. 'I'd have thought of something else.'

'I just bet you would,' Zanna muttered. She studied a non-existent fleck on her smooth fingernail. 'What I don't understand is—why.'

He was silent for a moment. Then, 'Perhaps I feel a certain—responsibility.'

'Because of what happened?' She made her tone derisive. 'We were both consenting adults. And I can't be the first one-night stand you've enjoyed.'

'It isn't something I make a habit of.' His voice had an edge to it.

'Should I feel honoured?'

'No,' he said. 'Although I suppose your feeling anything at all could be a major step forward.'

She winced inwardly, but rallied. 'If that's what you

think, I'm surprised you didn't leave me to my own devices.'

'Sometimes I surprise myself too,' he said grimly.

'Never mind,' Zanna said lightly. 'Tomorrow you'll be able to lay down your burden with a clear conscience.'

'Perhaps.'

'No,' she said. 'Definitely. Your stepmother may have all the charm in the world, but I'm out of here. You stick to controlling your galleries, Mr Lantrell, and leave me in peace. After all, if I'd wanted to be dominated and manipulated, I'd have stayed at Westcott Holdings.'

'You had a choice?' He sounded surprised.

'Doesn't everyone?'

'Not always,' Jake said slowly. 'And not from what I've heard of your father.'

'Well, now you know differently.' Zanna turned back to stare determinedly out of the car window. The scenery was spectacular, she had to admit. Tiny wisps of cloud swirled against the deep blue of the sky and the hills were an amalgam of bleached rock and purple shadow. On their lower slopes cypresses cast black shadows across the parched grass. It couldn't have been a greater contrast to the sophisticated bustle of the coast.

So wild, she thought. So isolated. And not somewhere you could leave in a hurry. A shiver ran through her.

'Are you cold? Is the air-conditioning too much?'

'No,' she said hurriedly. 'How much further is it?'

'About another kilometre.'

'And the house is called Les Étoiles—The Stars. Isn't that rather a strange name?'

Jake smiled faintly. 'You won't think so when you've spent a night there. When there are no clouds the stars look the size of a man's fist, and close enough to touch.'

Like at Emplesham. Repressing another shiver, Zanna

said coolly, 'I doubt if I'll be there long enough to notice.'

The car swung onto a dusty track with a downward gradient. Ahead of her Zanna could see a wall, and a pair of wrought-iron gates. As the car approached the gates swept open in obedience to a remote control device operated by Maurice, and closed behind them. It seemed there was no turning back.

There were more cypresses here, a whole avenue of them standing like silent sentinels, guarding the way down to the house. It lay in a hollow, a rambling cream-coloured building, two-storeyed, with a faded terracotta roof and green shutters masking the windows. It was big, but by no means as grand as Zanna had expected, and this was oddly reassuring.

As the car stopped in front of a short flight of shallow steps she turned to Jake to make some polite comment and saw that he was frowning, the firm mouth fixed and almost grim.

A woman in a dark dress had emerged from the main door of the house and was waiting for them.

'Madame Cordet,' Jake said quietly in response to Zanna's enquiring glance. 'I told you she existed.'

He put a hand firmly under her arm and escorted her up the steps.

The housekeeper's greeting was polite, but formal, and though her dark eyes were alive with curiosity she seemed ill at ease as she shook hands with Zanna.

'Et madame?' Jake asked abruptly, after he too had been greeted.

Madame Cordet's plump face looked anxious as she turned and led the way into the house.

After the radiance of the afternoon sun, the house was cool and full of shadows. Zanna was staring round her, trying to adjust to the change in light, when she became aware of a new and almost tangible tension in her companions. She saw that they were looking towards the wide sweep of staircase which dominated the hall.

At the bend of the stairs someone else was standing. A woman, Zanna saw, tall, with fair hair, and wearing a crimson blouse above a white skirt. In the dimness her face was a blur—apart from her eyes, which seemed to burn with a green flame as she looked down at them.

A stranger, but somehow as familiar as her own reflection. As familiar as the portrait that used to hang on her father's wall. Zanna felt suddenly as if she'd been turned to stone.

Her hand closed on Jake's arm. Her voice sounded hoarse, almost unrecognisable.

'Who—is that?'

'I think you know.'

His arm was behind her, urging her forward, gently but inexorably.

'No.' She tried to free herself, to run away, out into the sunshine. She wanted to escape from the shadows in this house. To turn her back on this incredible, this monstrous possibility. To recover her reeling sanity.

'It's all right.' He spoke softly, reassuringly. 'Darling, I swear to you everything will be all right.' He looked up at the woman on the stairs. 'Susan, my love, I've brought her to you at last.'

The woman put out shaking hands. 'Susie—my baby—my little blessed girl.' Her voice was deep and husky, cracking with emotion. Zanna was close enough now to see the tears glistening on her face.

Zanna turned on Jake. 'What is this? Another of your sick games? How dare you pretend that this is my mother? My mother's dead—she's been dead since I was a baby. Who is this woman? What's going on here?'

Jake put his hands on her shoulders and looked down

into her eyes. 'Listen to me, sweetheart.' His voice was gentle, but very firm. 'Your mother didn't die. That was a story your father invented to cover up the fact that she'd left him. To soothe his damned ego, he preferred to pretend she was dead rather than happy somewhere else without him.'

He added quietly, 'But she could never be completely happy, Susie. Not without you. All these years she's been waiting—praying for a chance to make contact with you.'

'No.' Zanna's voice broke. 'This can't be true—it can't. No one could do such a thing.'

'He wanted it to be true.' Susan Lantrell drew a deep, shuddering breath. 'Perhaps, eventually, he even came to believe it.'

'But all this time you let me believe it too,' Zanna cried out in anguish. 'How could you do that?'

'Because I was a coward,' the other woman said, with deep sadness.

Jake turned his head and spoke to the housekeeper, who was hovering, her face a mask of concern.

'Sylvie, make some tea, please, and bring it to the *salon*. I think we need to sit down calmly and talk this thing through.'

'Blame me if you want. Hate me if you must—but please, please listen to me,' Susan Lantrell added, with passionate intensity.

There was a long, troubled silence. So many thoughts were battling for supremacy in Zanna's tired brain. So many painful images, tumbling into her mind one after the other. So much that she now understood with anguished clarity.

She wanted to shut them off. To turn and walk away from it all. To wipe out all that had happened and revert to the single-minded, power-orientated girl she'd been only a couple of months ago. Before one reckless night had changed her life for ever.

But that, she knew, was impossible. That girl no longer existed. And, however much it might hurt, she realised she had to listen to what her mother had to say. Otherwise all the unanswered questions would remain with her for the rest of her life, like a wound that wouldn't heal.

Quietly she released herself from Jake's hands.

'Very well,' she agreed tonelessly. 'I'll listen.'

'I should never have married him,' said Susan Lantrell. Her eyes looked past Zanna, heavy with remembered suffering. 'I don't even know if I ever loved him. My mother was all for it, of course, because my father had left us rather badly off and Gerald had money.

'There *was* someone I wanted. His name was Peter, but he'd just started his own small engineering company and we couldn't even afford to get engaged. I was trying to establish myself as a painter, so I said I'd wait for him.'

'What happened?' Zanna asked. The *salon* was a large, high-ceilinged room, with long windows opening out on to a lawned garden. Above them a ceiling fan whirred languidly, providing a welcome breath of air.

She was seated on a deeply cushioned sofa. Jake was beside her and her mother sat opposite in a high-backed chair, her hands gripping its curved wooden arms as if she needed the support.

The tea had been placed on a table between them. It was hot and strong and it had stopped Zanna shaking inside.

'The company failed—was forced into receivership. It seemed to happen overnight. My mother said it was in-evitable, that Peter didn't have what it took to make a

go of anything. Afterwards he had a kind of breakdown.
I used to go and see him in hospital, but half the time
he didn't seem to know who I was. And I was under
this constant pressure—from my mother—from Gerald.'
She shook her head. 'It's no excuse, I know, but you
can't imagine what it was like.'

'Yes,' Zanna said quietly. 'Yes, I can.'

'I found myself married without quite knowing how
it had happened. In the end it seemed easier to give in
rather than keep fighting. We went to Jamaica for our
honeymoon. While we were there Gerald told me that
Peter was dead. That he'd killed himself. He told me as
if he was drawing a line under a balance sheet—writing
off some disappointing transaction.'

She looked soberly at Zanna. 'And it was then I knew
that the receivership had been his fault. That he'd used
his power, his contacts, to destroy Peter. I realised then
how far he was prepared to go to get what he wanted.'

She shuddered. 'I should have left him then, but perhaps I didn't want to admit that he could really be so
morally bankrupt. So—we came home, and I started
learning to be Lady Westcott. Everything—every aspect
of our lives—had to be subjugated to the success of
Westcott Holdings. He paraded me like a trophy—his
beautiful, talented young wife.

'Except that I didn't paint any more. Gerald resented
the time it took—the concentration that should have
been devoted to him. In private he began sneering at my
work, calling it ''Sue's daubs''. Publicly he referred to
it as if it was some pathetic little hobby, instead of an
essential part of me.

'Slowly I realised how completely he wanted to
change me. That everything that made me the person—
the woman—I was had to be erased from my memory
banks. He wanted a shell—a façade. Someone in a de-

signer dress who'd run his home like clockwork and never argue.'

'Was that when you painted that portrait of yourself?' Zanna asked quietly. 'The one without a face?'

Her mother nodded. 'It was a cry for help, but he couldn't see it. That was just before I found I was pregnant. He was furious about that too. He was just about to embark on a big Far Eastern trip, and the doctors said I couldn't go with him. He went on and on about the inconvenience, how stupid—how selfish I was.

'And then he started being very kind about it. Telling me that the doctors were worried about my general health—my emotional stability. That maybe this wasn't the right time to start a family. That perhaps we should think again.'

'Oh, God,' Zanna whispered, putting a hand to her mouth. 'Oh, dear God.' She felt Jake stir restively beside her.

Susan Lantrell looked down at her hands, clasped tensely in her lap. 'Perhaps I was stupid, but at first I really didn't see what he was getting at. When I realised, I was horrified. I waited till he'd gone to London, then I left the house and went to stay with my old nanny. I wrote to Gerald, saying I needed a break—a change of air—and that I'd see him when he came back from his trip.'

'Why didn't you leave him altogether?' Zanna asked. She was trembling again, and she felt Jake reach over and close a hand over hers.

'I intended to,' Susan said, with a sigh. 'I was going to ask him for a divorce. But when he returned he genuinely seemed to have changed. He was full of plans for when the baby was born—had rooms at the house turned into a nursery suite. I thought perhaps it was a turning point.'

Zanna said harshly, 'No one ever changes. Least of all my father.'

'When you were born, he was elated. On top of the world. I felt I had to give the marriage a second chance. But when I brought you home everything was different. I'd wanted my old nanny to be there to help me over the first weeks. Instead, Gerald had engaged a young woman I'd never met from one of the top agencies—all starch and timetables.'

Susan's mouth twisted wryly. 'She used to address me as "Mummy" and I hated her. Gerald insisted I gave up breastfeeding—too time-consuming, he said, and it would interfere with the nanny's routine. I had to take my place at his side again. You had your compartment. I had mine. And they were totally—totally separate.'

Zanna threw back her head. She said huskily, 'Was that why you found it so easy to leave me behind—when you left?'

'Easy?' Susan echoed, almost wonderingly. 'What are you talking about?' She got to her feet. 'You think it was *easy*?' Her voice rose.

Jake went swiftly over to her and put his arms round her. 'It's all right, Sue. Everything's going to be fine. We won't talk any more right now. I'll take Suzannah up to her room, get her settled in.'

'Thank you, Jake.' Susan made an effort to compose herself. 'Thank you for finding her. For bringing her to me.'

As they went up the stairs Zanna said savagely, 'Do you expect me to thank you too?'

'Maybe one day. But not now. You're in shock.'

'What is there to be shocked about? I've just discovered my father's been lying to me all my life and that if he'd had his way I'd probably never have been born at all. And, if that isn't enough, I also find that my mother, who was supposed to be dead, walked out on me and has been living in the lap of luxury in the South of France. Nothing to upset me at all.'

He said slowly, 'I know how you must be feeling…'

'No,' she said. 'No, you don't. I feel as if I've stepped through the looking glass into some nightmare.' She stopped. 'I—I can't stay here.'

'Just for tonight.' He opened a door, showed her into a room with apricot walls and a wide, low bed with an old-fashioned carved wooden headboard and a creamy coverlet embroidered with tiny roses. 'Don't judge until you've heard it all. Let her talk to you—tell you what happened.'

'I might do some talking of my own,' she said raggedly. 'Tell me something. At what point during my visit to Emplesham did you realise who I was?'

He hesitated. 'I wasn't sure at first, in spite of the similarity in colouring. But when you said your name…'

'Ah, yes,' she said. 'Big mistake. If I'd called myself "Jane" or "Vanessa" I'd probably have been allowed to go on my way unmolested.' She paused. 'Have you told your stepmother about all your sterling work on her behalf—checking me out to the nth degree? How you threw yourself into it—body and soul?'

He said wearily, 'It wasn't like that.'

'Shall we let her be the judge as to whether or not you could have found some way to tell me—to break the news—without the great seduction scene?'

'I was going to tell you,' he said. 'In the morning. But you left.'

She whistled. 'So it's my fault?' she exclaimed. 'Let me apologise for spoiling your cunning plan.'

'No,' he said quietly. 'The fault was entirely mine. I had no right to touch you. As I've already said, it was a wrong thing to have done and I've regretted it ever since.'

'Not,' she said, 'as much as I have. And now perhaps you'd go and let me have a rest. I have a feeling I'm going to need all my strength for the next thrilling instalment.'

He stood for a long moment, looking at her—a searing, contemptuous examination, which travelled from the top of her head down to her feet.

He said softly, 'While we're on the subject of regrets, Zanna, please don't give me cause to curse the day I ever saw you, let alone brought you here.'

He went out, closing the door behind him. Zanna stood rigidly for a moment. Then her face crumpled, she sank down onto the edge of the bed and began to cry.

CHAPTER TEN

A SHOWER in the small tiled bathroom which opened off her bedroom and a change of clothing made Zanna feel marginally better. At least on a physical level, she amended unhappily. Nothing could alleviate the emotional bruising she had undergone in the last few hours.

The part Jake had played she relegated to some locked, frozen compartment in her brain. She would deal with it when she was capable, she thought, flinching. But that was not yet.

She pulled a chair up to the window and sat down, resting her folded arms on the windowsill and staring out at the sunlit landscape.

Her first priority had to be her mother, of course. And what a ghastly irony it was that they should meet now, of all times, when it was impossible for her to maintain the relationship longer than a few weeks.

She'd examined her body intently in the long bathroom mirror, looking for tell-tale signs. Her waist hadn't thickened, as far as she could see, but already her breasts seemed marginally larger. Or was she imagining it? Whatever, pregnancy was not a secret anyone could keep for long.

Yet it was essential that no one in this house—*no one*—should guess what was happening to her. It would cause untold damage if the truth ever came out, Zanna told herself vehemently as she zipped herself into an ivory shift dress which managed to be chic and concealing at the same time.

Jake was clearly loved and trusted by Susan Lantrell,

whose own emotional fragility was obvious. What would it do to her if she discovered her long-lost daughter had been deliberately seduced by her stepson, whatever his motive might have been?

This was supposed to be a happy reunion, she thought, with a wry twist of her lips. The last thing she needed to do was blow an essentially close family relationship out of the water.

In a little while she'd be gone from all their lives. She'd already decided she had no choice about that. She would simply have to disappear, just as her mother had done all those years before. And Susan would need Jake's continuing affection and support in the wake of her departure. She couldn't say or do anything that would harm that.

The essential thing now was to find some realistic reason for distancing herself, without causing too much pain.

As for her own sense of loneliness and isolation, well, she would have to find a way of coming to terms with that, she thought, biting her lip.

She got restlessly to her feet. The room was spacious, but suddenly the walls seemed to be closing in on her. She needed the open air to breathe.

Quietly, she let herself out of her room and went downstairs. The house was very still. The doors to the *salon* stood open but the room was empty, and no one challenged her as she left the house.

She stood for a moment at the top of the steps, getting her bearings. From the window of her room, she'd seen formal gardens, and a glint of turquoise water which proclaimed a swimming pool. Common sense suggested that was where the family might congregate on such a glorious day, so she deliberately turned in the opposite direction.

Her route led her round the side of the house and under an archway into a cobbled yard, lined on three sides by ancient stone buildings, heavily timbered. Some of them had been turned into garaging for cars, but there was also a tall dovecote, busy with the flutter of white wings, and a row of loose boxes. As Zanna hesitated she could hear the sounds of movement and a soft whinny as a long muzzle and a pair of liquid dark eyes came into view.

'Oh, you beauty.' Gently Zanna stroked the velvety nose as the horse blew softly at her, questing hopefully for a titbit. It was a long time since she'd been near a horse. Not since Solomon, she thought with a pang, her beloved pony and inseparable companion until she'd gone to boarding school. She would never forget the dreadful start to the holidays when she'd come home and found the stable empty.

'Well, you'd outgrown him.' Her father had dismissed her sobbing protests. 'And he's gone to a good home,' he'd added unconvincingly.

Child though she was, Zanna had known that could not be true, that gentle, affectionate Solomon had been too elderly to find a ready sale.

'He could have stayed with us,' she'd wept. 'I'd have looked after him. He loved me. He wouldn't have been any trouble.'

'Absolute rubbish. You're away at school for most of the year, and you've got far more important things to concern you now than a geriatric pony.' Sir Gerald had been brusque. 'Anyway, animals should earn their keep. It's time you grew up, my dear.'

So she'd wept out her grief and then, with a resolution beyond her years, put Solomon out of her mind. And animals had become a taboo subject. She'd never asked for another horse, or even a dog or cat. There was less pain that way.

It was a lesson I should have remembered, she thought, feeling the horse's soft sweet breath on her face and neck. That anything or anyone is expendable once they've outlived their usefulness to my father. Was that something my mother discovered too?

The horse stirred restlessly under her caressing hand at the sound of approaching hooves, and Zanna realised someone had ridden under the archway into the courtyard.

The breath caught in her throat as she prayed it would not be Jake. She couldn't stand another confrontation, having to face him, having to pretend...

But as she turned slowly she saw that this was one prayer that hadn't been answered.

Jake swung himself lithely out of the saddle and came towards her, leading his handsome bay gelding.

'Looking for an escape route, Suzannah?' His smile mocked her. 'I wouldn't choose Celestine. Two kilometres from her stable and she turns and heads for home.'

'Thanks to your machinations, I'm going nowhere for the time being.' She kept her voice level.

He frowned. 'Is that all you can find to say? Does it mean nothing to have found your mother after all this time?'

'Of course it does,' she admitted reluctantly. 'But I still can't understand how anyone so apparently caring could just have turned her back on her own baby and walked away, whatever the problems. How she could have stayed away all these years without trying to get in touch—without giving me a thought.'

'My God,' he said softly. 'How little you know.'

For a moment Zanna felt seared by the contempt in

his dark eyes, then he turned from her abruptly, calling, 'Gustave,' and a short, bow-legged man promptly appeared from the tack room to take charge of the gelding.

Jake came towards her. Zanna stood her ground, determined not to flinch from the cold anger in his face.

'Come with me, my dear stepsister,' he said bitingly. 'I have something to show you.'

'No.' She hung back. 'This—this is a private matter—something for my mother and I to sort out on our own.'

'Oh, I think it's gone beyond that,' he shot back at her. 'Besides, I'm heavily involved already, remember?'

His hand was on her arm, harsh and implacable, urging her on towards the haystore in the corner of the yard.

'Where are we going?' Zanna tried to wrestle herself free.

'Not for a roll in the hay, anyway,' Jake returned tersely. 'That's a basic error I won't repeat.'

She said grittily, 'Well, at least we agree on one thing.'

She was being guided towards a flight of wooden steps, leading to an upper floor. As they climbed Zanna felt the familiar smells of oil paint and turpentine tangle in her throat.

They emerged into a massive L-shaped loft. It had been floored in immaculately varnished planking, and, beneath the high, raftered roof, whole sections of the wall had been removed and replaced with glass, flooding the entire space with clear, bright light.

Unframed canvases stood against the wall, and a half-finished local landscape waited on an easel.

Zanna drew a breath as she looked around her. 'Does your father provide my mother with a studio in every house they occupy?'

'Yes,' he said, with unsmiling curtness.

'Well, that explains it. She obviously left me to find

herself—no sacrifice too great for her art?' Under the bitterness there was a tremor in her voice.

Jake swore under his breath. 'I'm not a violent man,' he said, too quietly. 'I've never hit anyone in my life, or particularly wanted to. But in your case, Ms Westcott, I'm sorely tempted to make an exception—to put you across my knee and paddle you till you squirm.'

She sent him a glittering smile. 'Very unwise, Mr— er—Lantrell, or whatever current identity you're using.' She took another look round. 'I presume you have another purpose in bringing me here?'

'I have a purpose. But I'm not sure any more if there's a point. You've got a closed mind, Suzannah. You're not prepared to make any kind of concession, are you?'

'I might have listened,' she said. 'That night in Emplesham. But you seemed to want a different kind of concession then.'

His mouth tightened. 'I've already told you how much I regret that. Do you want me to grovel? Or shall we agree it was a combination of too much wine and moonlight, and write it off as a mutual mistake?'

'Mutual?' Her head went back, challenging him.

'Entirely,' he came back at her, with emphasis. 'You wanted me as much as I wanted you, so don't try and pretend otherwise.'

Aware she was on shaky ground, Zanna switched tack. 'You didn't think you should have mentioned that we were related?'

'Not to any degree that mattered.' He paused. 'Nor was it my secret to tell. You and your father were still together, personally and professionally, and I could say nothing without consulting Susan—getting her permission.'

'Was that really so necessary?'

'Yes,' he said levelly. 'Oh, yes.'

He moved over to one stack of canvases and, kneeling, began turning them over. 'Now, come and look at these.'

Reluctantly she knelt beside him. Then, 'They're all Church House,' she said, surprised. 'All the same picture, over and over again.'

'Look more closely,' he said. 'And you'll see they're all marginally different.'

'Yes.' Zanna peered, frowning. 'Yes, I see now.' She pointed. 'In this one there's a pram in the garden. And in the next there's a child: a little girl in a blue dress, playing with a dog—and then the same child, on a pony…' Her voice tailed away as she absorbed what she was seeing. What she was saying.

He said gently, 'And in this one she's in school uniform. And here she is all grown up.'

'No,' she almost shouted. She sat back on her heels, wrapping her arms defensively round her body. She said, 'The child in all the pictures—it's me, isn't it?'

'Yes,' he said. 'It was the only way she could keep close to you—by imagining you at every stage in the life she'd lost out on.' His voice deepened. 'There wasn't a day she didn't think about you or want you. You have to know that—to believe it.'

'Then why did she go?' she whispered thickly, through the tightness in her throat. 'If she had to leave, why didn't she take me with her—her own child?'

'She tried,' Jake said quietly. 'When she couldn't bear it any more—the bullying, the humiliations, the continual denigration—when she realised her sanity was on the line, she knew she had to go. So, she packed as much as she could, put you in a carrying cot and left the house one morning as soon as it was daylight. She left your father a note telling him she couldn't go on and she'd give him a divorce.'

He paused. 'She was trying to get to Grace Moss's house, going across country, using minor roads. But he tracked her somehow, caught her near a patch of woodland—forcing her car off the road.'

Zanna cried out, a hand going to her appalled face as she registered what he'd said.

'The car hit a tree and she blacked out for a moment. When she recovered consciousness she could hear you crying. He was standing by the car, looking in at her, holding your cot.'

He shook his head. 'Susan says she'll never forget his voice—the look in his eyes. Or his words. She's repeated them so often, I know them by heart. He said, ''You can go, Susan, and be damned to you. As a wife, you're no use to me. But you're not taking the child. You got off lightly this time because she was in the car, but if you ever come near either of us again I'll destroy you, and that's a promise. From this moment on, you're a dead woman anyway.'''

'Oh, God.' Zanna found she was rocking backwards and forwards. 'Oh, no, how could he?'

But she already knew what her father was capable of. She'd seen his self-obsession and ruthlessness. Felt its ruinous effects on her own life. Wasn't that why she was here now—for good or ill?

Jake went on, 'She watched him drive away, taking you with him. She was dazed, but she still couldn't have moved—couldn't have stopped him—because she knew he meant every word. She was just too frightened to stop him, and that's what she's blamed herself for ever since. That's the guilt he's made her live with. That she was too much of a coward to risk everything—to fight him for you.'

Her lips moved painfully. 'It wasn't cowardice, it was self-preservation. Believe me, I know.'

Jake took her by the shoulders and turned her to face him. 'What made you split from him, Susie?'

His touch made a thousand sensations coruscate inside her. The bright air seemed to swirl around them, charged and alive with a strange energy into which the distant cooing of the doves added an extra rhythmic dimension. She felt the radiance, the pulsation quivering in her veins, tingling on her nerve-endings. If she had not been kneeling, she thought, she might have fallen to the ground.

She stared up into the dark face, remembering how it had been with them during the long intensity of that night together. Remembering his mouth warm and sensuous on her heated skin. Remembering his eyes, heavy with passion, then lit with a sudden flame as he lost control.

No passion, now, in his gaze, but an infinite tenderness which reached into her inmost being, lighting the darkness there, warming the deathly cold she carried like a stone.

It would be so easy to tell him about the baby—here, at this moment. To put her mouth on his and take his hands and draw them to her belly.

So easy—and so impossible. It was the last news on earth that he would want to hear at such a time. Or ever, for that matter.

She shrugged deliberately, making him relax his hold, release her. 'Oh, a combination of things.' She paused. 'Maybe I'm more my mother's daughter than I knew, and I needed to save my soul.'

Jake watched her expressionlessly for a moment, then got to his feet. He said, 'I hope you have a speedier salvation than Susan's. It took a long time before my father could persuade her that she was safe—that she could afford to love, to trust. And that she herself deserved to be loved and trusted in turn. Give her a chance, Susie,' he added quietly. 'Don't hurt her again. And give yourself a chance too.'

She didn't want to meet his gaze. She couldn't afford to expose herself to that tenderness, that concern again. It was too dangerous. That same tenderness had beguiled her once with disastrous results. She couldn't let it happen again, however great the temptation, however burning the need to let his arms close round her, to sink into his embrace and feel her body trembling against his.

She looked past him. Her voice was light, almost brittle. 'You keep mentioning your father, but he doesn't seem to be around.'

Jake sighed swiftly and harshly. 'He's been in Paris. But he'll be back this evening.'

She nodded brightly. 'I shall look forward to meeting him. Now, if you wouldn't mind, I'd like to be on my own for a while.'

He said tonelessly, 'Of course.'

She heard him descend the wooden stairs, then there was silence.

For a moment she stayed very still, her eyes shut so tightly that brilliant sparks danced against her lids.

Then, very slowly, she began to go through the canvases again, examining and re-examining all the tiny changing details that had made up her imagined childhood. Trying to understand what had been going through her mother's mind as she constantly recreated for her lost daughter the timeless safety of that sunlit garden where she herself had been happy.

Perhaps, thought Zanna, she felt it would keep me safe. And maybe it did, at that.

Her attention was alerted by the faint rustle of silk, a fragrance of lilies and jasmine in the air, and, glimpsed out of the corner of her eye, a flash of indigo.

She turned abruptly to find Susan standing a few yards away. She was wearing a kaftan, exquisitely embroidered with butterflies, and she looked equally as fragile and ephemeral.

Zanna scrambled to her feet, still clutching one of the canvases, feeling an intruder.

She said awkwardly, 'Jake brought me here—he showed me...'

Her mother nodded. 'I know. He said you wanted to be alone, but I wondered—I hoped...'

Across the space that separated them, across the lonely years, Zanna saw the crippling uncertainty, the tense fear of rejection. She held out the canvas she was holding. The one with the child on horseback.

She said, 'There was a pony. His name was Solomon and I loved him. My father got rid of him too.'

She saw the taut face crumple, felt her own rigidity drain out of her. The picture fell unheeded to the floor as she took one step, then another, until she reached her mother's arms.

CHAPTER ELEVEN

DINNER that night was a festive occasion.

Zanna and Susan had spent two hours sitting on the floor of the studio together, talking, laughing and crying too, because there was pain to share as well as happiness.

To Zanna's relief, her mother had not probed too deeply into the reasons behind her breach with Sir Gerald, accepting Zanna's explanation that she had come to see him, finally, for what he was, and had not been able to bear it.

Which, Zanna thought wanly, was not so far from the truth. She had also given her mother a brief and drastically expurgated version of her meeting with Jake.

In return, she'd learned that on her eventual arrival at Grace Moss's house Susan had suffered a nervous collapse and spent months in hospital. When she'd recovered she had gone abroad, visiting firstly an old schoolfriend who had settled in Portugal.

'Veronica and her husband were wonderful,' Susan said simply. 'They convinced me I had a reason to go on living—and they started me painting again. I thought, with everything that had happened, I might have lost it.'

She lifted her head proudly, 'Instead I realised I had a means of earning my living, if nothing else. I sold landscapes to tourists and took private painting classes—anything that would earn money.'

She drew a breath. 'And, as soon as it was legally possible, I divorced Gerald without his consent.'

'So how did you meet Mr Lantrell?' Zanna asked carefully.

Susan laughed. 'During one of my classes. I was working in France and I'd been asked to teach a course at Arles. I'd taken my group to one of the local markets to sketch and Gordon was walking past. He came over to look at some of the work, and—that was it.

'He had incredible patience,' she added tenderly, 'because I was determined not to get involved. I suppose I knew as soon as I saw him, but fought my feelings for him every step of the way. But in the end he won. He always does.' She smiled. 'It's a trait Jake shares.'

'Yes.' Zanna picked up one of the canvases and studied it with minute concentration. He wouldn't win this time, she promised herself fiercely. She wouldn't allow it.

By the time Madame Cordet arrived to say scoldingly that *monsieur* had returned from Paris and dinner was being served—on the instant—the studio was full of evening shadows.

Gordon Lantrell was waiting at the door for them, the laughter lines beside his mouth deepening tenderly as he surveyed his radiant wife.

He was, Zanna realised with a pang, exactly what Jake would be in another thirty years. Tall, and still lean, with his mane of dark hair greying at the temples. Dynamic, humorous, and still heart-stoppingly attractive.

Only she would not be there to see it, she reminded herself, pinning her smile on ever more firmly. And no one but herself knew how agonisingly short-lived this entire reunion was going to be.

But she wouldn't think about that now, she told herself, coming back to the present as a champagne cork popped and her glass was filled. Tonight she would enjoy herself. Tomorrow she would consider ways of extricating herself from this impossible situation.

'I want to drink a toast,' Susan Lantrell said softly.

'To all the people I love best in the world, gathered now around this table.' Her luminous smile touched each one in turn.

She turned to Zanna. 'It took a couple of years after Gordon bought Church House for me to pluck up the courage to go back there. But, when I did, I used to imagine that I would look out of the window one day and see you walking up the path towards me.'

'And then, when I did, you weren't there.' In her own ears Zanna's voice sounded over-bright. 'Instead there was only Jake, who thought I was a burglar casing the joint—or worse.'

'I don't believe I knew what to think.' Jake's hooded gaze met hers across the candlelit table. 'In many ways I still don't,' he added softly.

Zanna leaned back in her chair and took a sip from her glass to ease a suddenly dry mouth.

The food was delicious. A delicate seafood bisque was followed by a vegetable terrine, and then lamb cooked with garlic and rosemary was served with tiny peas and potatoes. A platter of cheeses was served on vine leaves, and finally, for dessert, an apricot tart with meltingly rich sweet pastry.

'I couldn't eat another thing,' Zanna laughingly declined as Madame Cordet urged her to another slice of tart. 'I've eaten enough for two already...'

Her voice halted abruptly as she realised what she'd said. A wave of colour heated her face and she leaned back in her chair, glad of the shadowed privacy that the candlelight afforded, praying that her momentary glitch hadn't been noticed.

Susan was talking, happily oblivious to her daughter's confusion. 'Oh, I've got such plans, Susie. I can't wait to start showing you off to our friends.' She smiled at her husband. 'Darling—we'll give a party.'

'Great idea, honey. But maybe we should give Suzannah a chance to settle in—find her feet before we do any major entertaining.' He paused. 'After all, we've all the time in the world.'

Zanna touched the tip of her tongue to her dry lips. 'Not all that much time, actually,' she said quietly. 'It's wonderful to be here, of course, but I can't stay around for ever. I—I do have to earn my living.'

'Oh, but you will,' Susan said eagerly. 'We didn't get you here on completely false pretences. I really have been commissioned to write a book—a popular guide to the painters who've been inspired by the South of France.' She pulled a comical face. 'Nothing very erudite, or up-market, but it should be fun to do. And Solange has had to leave to look after her mother, so I do need secretarial back-up.' She spread her hands, smiling. 'And when she comes back I'm sure your business experience would be invaluable in the Lantrell Gallery network. So—all problems solved.'

Zanna cast a fleeting glance from under her lashes at Jake, but he too was leaning back in his chair, and his expression was unreadable.

'Well, not exactly,' she said carefully. 'I thought this was just a—a temporary post, so I've—committed myself elsewhere.'

'Going back to the rat-race, Suzannah?' Jake's voice goaded from the shadows.

'Not in the way you think,' Zanna retorted, improvising frantically. 'A girl I was at school with has set up a head-hunting company and she wants me to join her. There's the possibility of a partnership. It's just too good to turn down.'

There was a silence, then, 'Well, naturally you have to consider your career,' Susan acknowledged sadly.

'Although I'm very disappointed.' She paused. 'Just as long as this job doesn't take you too far away.'

Zanna pushed away her empty plate. 'I'm afraid it does.' She felt as if a fist had closed on her heart, twisting it. 'It's in Australia.'

She felt the shock tremor run round the table. Then, 'Which part?' Jake asked.

Zanna stiffened. Had Lantrell Galleries established an Australian base? If so, it was likely to be in Sydney or Melbourne, she thought, trying desperately to remember what Megan had said.

She lifted her chin. 'Brisbane,' she said.

'Well, that's about as far away as it's possible to get,' Jake agreed silkily. 'Except for Darwin.'

'Then we'll just have to make the most of the time we've got,' Susan said, clearly trying to speak bravely. 'What's your friend's name, darling?'

Zanna cast her mind swiftly back to her sixth form days. 'Caroline,' she said. 'Caroline Phillips.'

She was thankful when she could at last plead fatigue and get away to her room. She hadn't been granted an easy passage, she thought ruefully as she went upstairs. The cross-examination had been loving from her mother, shrewd and concerned from her new stepfather, and intense from both of them.

Jake, however, had asked nothing at all, his whole attention apparently concentrated on the cognac he'd been allowing to swirl gently in the bowl of his glass. She could have sworn he hadn't drunk one drop, and this, in some odd way, was more disturbing than any inquisition would have been.

Perhaps he realised that 'Check' had finally been called in this strange game they'd been playing.

And if he was secretly planning to keep tabs on her in Australia he'd be unlucky, she told herself, squaring her shoulders as she went into her room. By the time he realised she'd never gone to Brisbane she would be safely ensconced in the north of England, with the trail—hopefully—cold behind her.

She wanted to sleep. She wanted to close her eyes and blot out the hurt and disappointment in Susan Lantrell's face. She wanted to lose in unconsciousness all the shocks and bewilderment of the past twenty-four hours, but sleep was elusive. She lay, staring into the sultry darkness, her mind on an endless treadmill, pursued by one image after another.

But it was Jake's image that predominated, in spite of her best efforts to banish him. She felt his teasing smile like a kiss on her starved lips, his dark gaze like a caress on her aching flesh.

So close, she thought painfully. And yet beyond her reach for ever. The lover of one night transformed into friend and even surrogate brother. Which was the last thing she wanted.

The thin coverlet was oppressive, twining round her limbs, anchoring her restless body to the bed. Moonlight, pouring through the shutters, lay in silver bars across the floor, reinforcing the impression that she was in a cage of her own making.

Feeling suddenly suffocated, Zanna freed herself, swinging her feet to the floor and reaching for her robe. Her mouth was dry, she thought. That was why she couldn't sleep. She was simply thirsty. She needed something cold to drink—fruit juice, or a mineral water.

Moving as quietly as possible, she let herself out of her room and padded downstairs.

The door to the *salon* was standing ajar, but she went past it without hesitation, finding her way to the big kitchen at the back of the house. Here, everything was calmness and order, she reflected almost wistfully, looking round her at the enormous dresser occupying the whole of one wall, the well-scrubbed table in the middle of the room, the array of polished pans and utensils, all bathed in the brightness of the moonlight.

She took a glass from the drying rack then opened the cavernous fridge and extracted a bottle of Evian water. She was struggling to remove the cap when the kitchen light suddenly went on.

She cried out in shock, catching her foot in her robe as she tried to turn, feeling the glass slip from her hand and smash to pieces on the flagged floor.

Jake said harshly, 'So it was you, creeping round in the dark. I thought it must be. That, or a ghost.'

'I—I'm very much alive. I just wanted a drink.' She stood, clutching the bottle against her as if it were a shield. 'I—I didn't mean to wake anyone.'

'I haven't been to bed.' He came to where she was standing, his hands firm on her waist as he lifted her clear of the broken glass in one swift, summary movement and deposited her on the edge of the table. 'Stay there while I clear up the mess.'

'I can manage—' she began, to be silenced by his derisive glance.

'And end up with glass in your foot? I don't want anything else to feel guilty about.'

She sat, mute, watching as he dealt quickly and deftly with the shards. He was still fully dressed, she saw, in the elegantly cut dark trousers he'd been wearing at dinner and the ivory silk shirt, open at the neck, cuffs turned back to reveal tanned forearms. For her part Zanna felt absurdly vulnerable in her thin robe, bare feet dangling.

'Thank you,' she said stiltedly, when he'd finished. 'I'd better take my drink back to my room. I don't want to cause any more problems.'

His brows lifted sardonically. 'You surprise me. Was

it really the pangs of thirst keeping you awake, or your conscience?'

Zanna stiffened. 'What do you mean? It's never easy to sleep under a strange roof.'

'Or,' he said softly, 'in a strange bed.'

Zanna felt the colour rise in her face, but she made herself meet the faint mockery in his eyes.

'Or that either,' she agreed equably, and slid off the table. 'Perhaps it would be safer if I looked for a paper cup.'

'I don't think you'll find one.' He paused. 'On the other hand,' he went on silkily, 'you could consider a different cure for insomnia.'

His smile widened as he heard her swift, betraying intake of breath.

'What are you talking about?' she demanded raggedly.

He shrugged. 'I was going to offer you a *tisane*. Madame Cordet uses them as a sovereign remedy for everything.'

'A *tisane*?' she said uncertainly.

He nodded laconically. 'A herbal drink. Guaranteed to soothe troubled nerves. Not that you seem to suffer from them,' he added, his mouth twisting. 'Aren't you even the slightest bit concerned about the effect of your recent bombshell?'

She bit her lip. 'Of course I am. I regret it very much. But, under the circumstances, I had no choice. I could hardly let my mother start making plans for the future— imagining us all as one big happy family—when I knew it couldn't happen.'

'So, when did you actually arrive at this epoch-making decision?' His tone was casual as he filled the kettle and set it on the stove, but she wasn't fooled for a minute, all her warning systems in overdrive.

She said brightly, 'Oh, Caroline suggested I should join her ages ago, but I was still settled at Westcott Holdings at the time.'

'And now you've been allowed a second chance.' Jake sent her a meditative look. 'Not everyone's so fortunate.'

'I'm the lucky one all right,' she agreed, with terrible irony.

'And your good luck is Susan's misfortune.' He busied himself for a moment, collecting two glass beakers in attractive metal holders from a cupboard in the dresser. When he spoke again, his voice was cool and level. 'Would you be prepared to think again?'

Zanna was replacing the Evian water in the fridge. Her head turned sharply. 'I—I don't understand.'

'Yes, you do.' He was opening and closing a set of miniature drawers situated at one side of the dresser, choosing two small packets like teabags. 'I suspect that your sudden decision to go to—Darwin…?'

'Brisbane,' she supplied curtly.

'Could have been sparked off by my presence here.' Jake threw back his head in an oddly defenceless gesture. 'What I'm trying to say is—that doesn't have to be a problem for you. For either of us.'

Zanna's fingers twisted nervously in the skirts of her robe. 'You mean—you'd—go?'

He nodded. 'You don't have to disappear to the other side of the world—or anywhere—to get away from me.' There was a trace of bitterness in his voice. 'With a little forward planning, we should be able to avoid each other pretty well.'

She said slowly, 'Jake—I'm the outsider. I don't want to drive you out of your own home.'

'And I don't want to see a woman I love and respect breaking her heart because she's caught in the middle of our private war,' he returned brusquely. 'Agreed, it's not an ideal solution, but it could ease the situation.'

'Not,' she said, 'for your father. He has to be considered.'

'Dad's not a fool. He's already picked up on the fact there are tensions between us. I imagine you don't want him launching an enquiry into the causes?'

She said hurriedly, 'No—oh, no.'

'And fortunately Lantrell Galleries operate worldwide. There'll be no shortage of excuses for me to be elsewhere.' He poured boiling water into the beakers and left the *tisanes* to infuse. 'Well, is it a deal?'

Zanna felt deathly cold. 'I—I don't know. I've only just got my independence. I—I can't surrender it so soon—walk into another place that's been prepared for me.'

'Isn't that what you'll be doing in Brisbane?'

For a second she stared at him, her hastily concocted story a thousand miles from her mind. She recovered herself just in time.

'Not exactly. Caro wants to expand her business,' she invented wildly. 'So I'll be boxing my own corner. It won't be a free ride to this kind of privilege.'

His mouth twisted. 'You don't approve of privilege? You've undergone a sea change since our first meeting. You were the most imperious thing since Catherine the Great.'

She didn't meet his gaze. 'Perhaps I've gained a different perspective since then.'

'Or had it forced upon you,' he said drily.

'That, too.' Zanna held out her hand. 'Thank you for the *tisane*. I look forward to trying it.'

'I'll take it to your room.' Jake lifted the beaker carefully. 'Drop this, and you could end up scalded.'

'I don't,' she said, 'make a habit of breaking things.'

'No?' His smile was swift and bleak. 'You could have fooled me.'

Their glances met, clashed, then Zanna turned and swept from the room with as much dignity as her bare feet would allow.

She was hotly aware that he was close behind her on the stairs. On the landing he walked past her, opened her door, and motioned her to precede him with a courtly gesture.

Heart thumping, but head high, Zanna obeyed. She retreated to the window in the pretext of fiddling with the drapes, conscious of his every movement. Not that he was doing anything particularly alarming—just switching on her lamp, setting the beaker down on the night-table. And going.

As he reached the doorway she halted him. 'Jake. About what you were saying downstairs...' She paused, touching her tongue to her dry lips. 'I—I don't know. Wouldn't it be better if we both just made an effort for the time remaining? Tried to—get along with each other somehow?'

He shook his head. 'I'm afraid that isn't possible.'

'But why not?'

'Do I really have to spell it out?' His voice startled her with its sudden raw savagery.

She didn't even see him move, but there he was, beside her, reaching for her. She felt his fingers twist in the silkiness of her hair, his other hand cupping her throat, forcing her mouth up to meet his with stark urgency. As their lips met she heard a roaring in her ears, felt a pulsation in her veins as old and primitive as the earth itself.

There was no past, she recognised in some hidden corner of her mind. There could be no future. There was only now, and the fire and honey of Jake's kiss.

He wasn't gentle, but she was too famished for the taste and touch of him to require more subtlety or consideration. Her own need was fierce—overwhelming. As their mouths strained together Zanna felt Jake's hips grind against hers in overt demand, conquering her grace with his strength. Her soft moan was a cry of yearning—a plea for assuagement.

He pushed the robe away from her shoulders, baring her to the waist. She arched herself back over his supporting arm, offering him her breasts, their rosy peaks already hardening in greedy anticipation.

For a moment he seemed to hover above her, his mouth a fraction of an inch from her tumescent flesh, and she realised that he was breathing the scent of her skin as if it were some new and erotic incense.

Then, at last, when every nerve-ending seemed to be screaming at him to put her out of this torment, he bent to her, and she felt the faint roughness of his cheek on her body as he suckled from her, deeply and languorously, his tongue a delicate flame flickering on her nipple.

She buried her face in the curve of his neck and shoulder, licking away a salt droplet of sweat, her mouth tugging at his taut skin. She felt drugged—intoxicated by his nearness, her senses at fever-pitch.

His hand parted the skirts of her robe, seeking the secret heated moisture of her, assuring himself of her readiness—her acceptance.

As he lifted her fully into his arms to carry her to the bed Zanna heard herself sigh in pleasure and anticipation. Her arms wound round his neck and her mouth sought his softly, but with sensuous emphasis.

Jake put her down on the mattress and leaned over her, stroking the edges of the robe completely apart as if unwrapping a longed-for gift. His eyes glittered down at her. He was trembling, holding onto his control with a supreme effort.

'Lovely,' he whispered. 'You're so lovely, darling. Even more glorious than before.'

His fingers, tracing a questing path down her body from breast to hip, lingered for a moment on the faint swell of her stomach.

And with that one, simple gesture he brought her crashing back to reality.

The baby, she thought with sudden anguish. The doctor had said that lovemaking could be dangerous in the early months. That she should be careful.

She'd dismissed the warning as irrelevant in her case. Yet here she was again—seduced, spellbound and ready to give herself. Only she dared not—not if there was even a remote chance of putting at risk the tiny life she was sheltering.

She would have to tell him—to explain—whatever the consequences. There would never, she thought, be a better moment.

As he lifted himself away from her to remove his own clothes Zanna sat up, reaching out a staying hand.

She said, on a little sob, 'Jake—no. I can't. We—we mustn't...' Her words tailed away as she tried to think— to find the right words.

There was a silence, then he sighed, briefly and harshly, turning his head away as if he could not bear to look at her.

'No,' he said. 'Indeed we must not insult your mother and my father in this way. Thank you for the badly needed reminder.' Moving to the edge of the bed, he began to refasten his shirt.

'Listen, please.' She gripped his arm. 'You don't understand...'

'Yes, I do.' Jake detached himself from her clasp. His

voice was bleak, his unsmiling face that of a stranger. 'I understand only too well. This is what I was trying to tell you only a few moments ago.'

'No,' Zanna almost wailed. 'You've got to let me explain.'

Jake shook his head, placing a silencing finger on her parted lips. 'Explanations are unnecessary and excuses impossible. What happened between us in England was a serious mistake. I had no right to behave as I did—no right at all. And any repetition would be a disaster.'

He drew a deep breath. 'So, I have to leave, Suzannah, because I can't trust myself to share a roof with you.' He gave a small, harsh laugh. 'I seem to be addicted to you, and that's something I can't afford.'

He got to his feet. 'They say the best cure for addiction is to go cold turkey. So I shall. Starting tomorrow.'

At the door, he turned and looked at her, his gaze impersonal, almost clinical.

'Don't forget your *tisane*. It's supposed to bring you deep sleep and sweet dreams.' His mouth twisted. 'I really hope it works—for both our sakes. Goodnight, Susie—and goodbye.'

And the door closed behind him with quiet finality.

CHAPTER TWELVE

'SUCH a shame that Jake had to leave,' Susan said over breakfast the next morning. 'I hoped so much that he'd stay—spend some time with us all.' She glanced at Zanna, whose eyes were fixed on her plate. 'I do want you both to be friends.'

'He'll be back soon, sweetheart,' her husband said comfortingly. 'Just as soon as he's got things sorted out in London.'

Susan sighed. 'I suppose so, but sometimes I worry that he's turning into a workaholic. That there's nothing else in his life but the galleries and those classic cars of his.'

'He'll change when the right woman comes along.' Gordon Lantrell grinned at his wife. 'I did.'

'But when's that going to be?' Susan fretted.

Gordon's look was droll. 'Maybe when he's finished having fun with the wrong ones.' He took his wife's hand and kissed it lightly. 'Something tells me it'll be for Jake like it was with us. One look—one touch—and he'll know for sure and for ever.'

'I hope so.' Susan brightened. 'And he's promised faithfully to make it back here for the party.'

That wasn't what she wanted to hear, Zanna thought unhappily, reducing her croissant to inedible crumbs. If she was ever to recover her peace of mind she needed him to stay away, and as far as possible, until she, herself, could make her escape.

Rather to her surprise, the lukewarm *tisane* had produced the desired effect the previous night, and, in spite

161

of her emotional turmoil and aching senses, she had
fallen deeply asleep. And if her dreams had not been
sweet at least they'd left no unhappy traces in her psyche
either.

A searching look in the mirror this morning had revealed that she was still pale and slightly hollow-eyed,
but relatively composed.

In retrospect, she could only be thankful that Jake had
prevented her from speaking—from telling him about
the baby. He would never know that the 'serious mistake' had already turned into a disaster. But at least it
had underlined for her, irrevocably and without ambi-
guity, that he looked back with nothing but regret on the
night they'd spent together.

Whereas she, with all the difficulties and loneliness of
single motherhood to face, regretted nothing. Now
there's an irony, she told herself. Because she knew now,
with total certainty, exactly what spell Jake had cast over
her that night—the spell of love.

And that, she thought fiercely, made it all worthwhile,
even though the love was all on her side and not his.

She knew that even if she had the time over again she
wouldn't forego one moment of their brief night together, or lose any of the bitter-sweet memories which
were all she'd have to take with her into the future.

But everything she'd just heard at the breakfast table
reinforced her need to get away as soon as possible. She
could endure a great deal, she told herself, but not the
heartbreak of seeing Jake finally fall in love with someone else.

Days passed and turned into a week, and then another,
and still Jake stayed away. In spite of the sad ache in
her heart, and her ever-present guilt over the secret she
could not tell, Zanna found herself relaxing and settling

almost insensibly into the gentle routine of life at Les Étoiles.

Most days she worked with Susan on the projected book. Much of their time was spent in travelling round the region, armed with a pocket tape-recorder and a camera, visiting some of the places which had inspired Van Gogh, Picasso, Matisse and Renoir. She was thrilled to find that Paul Cézanne's studio in Aix had been lovingly preserved, right down to his cape and beret hanging in a corner and glasses and a bottle on the table.

In the evenings she transcribed Susan's ideas from tape to computer or swam in the pool, relishing the coolness of the water after the sultry heat of the day.

At other times she went with her mother and Gordon into Cannes or Nice. In spite of her protests, an account with a generous deposit—'Advance salary,' Susan had excused it—had been opened for her in a local bank. In addition, they'd insisted on buying her a dress for the forthcoming party in one of the boutiques along the Croisette.

In the end she'd allowed herself to be persuaded into an ivory silk ankle-length shift, saved from demureness by the skirt, slashed almost to the thigh at one side. But she'd been shocked to find that her dress size had already increased from a ten to a twelve, although she'd managed laughingly to blame Sylvie Cordet's cooking. She only hoped the gown would still fit by the night of the party.

The kitchen at Les Étoiles had become one of her favourite places. She'd had little time or inclination for cooking up to then, and to watch Madame Cordet serenely and skilfully preparing the family's meals was a revelation.

The best and freshest ingredients, *madame* told her

with a broad smile, should be treated with complete simplicity, and then—*voilà*—everything arranged itself.

Observing *madame* chopping herbs with a fearsomely sharp knife, boning meat or stirring some delectably fragrant stockpot, Zanna thought, wryly, that there might be a little more to it than that.

She'd also paid several visits, under Gordon's guidance, to the Lantrell Gallery in Nice, where her arrival had caused a discreet stir. She'd received, in addition, a complex and thorough breakdown on how the galleries as a whole operated.

Gordon, she realised ruefully, was trying to woo her to his cause—convince her that here lay a far better career opportunity than any personnel recruitment service on the other side of the world. And under any other circumstances she would have agreed, would have been eager to take the place on the team that was clearly on offer.

The thought of leaving them all—of cutting herself off from all this warmth and affection—was almost unbearable. Just as the thought of never seeing Jake again was wholly unbearable.

She could fill the days, but her nights were torment. She was thankful when the moon began to wane and her bedroom was no longer aglow with that evocative silver light. It was easier to hide in the darkness from her thoughts—from her memories.

The arrangements for the party proceeded smoothly. Susan had specified on the invitations that guests were being asked to meet her daughter, and there had been few refusals.

'Everyone will be mad with curiosity,' Susan commented over lunch a week beforehand as she checked through some late acceptances.

'You don't mind that?'

'Darling, I'm too happy to mind anything. I'm just praying you'll meet someone wonderful on the night and decide you can't bear to tear yourself away.'

Zanna forced a smile. 'Well, you never know...' She hesitated. 'Can I do anything to help—prepare some of the food, maybe?'

Susan shook her head. 'I always use an outside firm. They do the food, the decorations, provide the music—everything. They're wonderful. And, more important, Gordon doesn't get upset.'

'Doesn't he like parties?'

'Loves them,' Susan said fondly. 'He's the most indulgent husband, and a marvellous host, but he hates the ordinary household routine being turned on its head for days beforehand. And if Sylvie stopped cooking his meals in favour of party food he'd be distraught.'

At that point the man in question came in, looking pleased. 'That was Jake on the phone, honey. He's arriving tonight and bringing Cindy Wybrandt with him.' He sat down, unfolding his napkin.

Under the edge of the table Zanna's hands were clenched suddenly together, her nails scoring ridges into her palms.

'Oh?' Susan raised her eyebrows. 'Is that on again?'

'Seems so—if it was ever off.' Gordon chuckled. 'Jake plays his cards close to his chest where his romantic involvements are concerned.' He broke off to sniff rapturously at the contents of the tureen which Madame Cordet had just placed in front of him.

'Well, she's a beautiful girl,' he went on, ladling the soup into bowls, 'and Abe Wybrandt is one of our most distinguished clients. He could do a lot worse.'

'Indeed he could.' Susan returned his smile. 'Maybe the next party I plan will be for his wedding.'

It was a hideous meal. Zanna had no appetite whatsoever, but she forced herself to eat and show her usual appreciation. Anything less would have been dangerously near to self-betrayal.

When lunch was over, she excused herself and went up to her room. She lay on the bed, staring up at the ceiling, her thoughts churning wildly.

So that was the underlying reason for all Jake's bitter regrets. He was already seriously committed elsewhere, and to a relationship he wasn't prepared to jeopardise any further, whatever the temptation.

Dress it up as he might, all she'd been to him was a brief divergence off the straight and narrow path leading to engagement and a suitable marriage.

And men were so easily diverted, she thought bitterly. Wasn't that part of the wisdom you were supposed to acquire at your mother's knee—that casual sex meant nothing to them, and they wouldn't respect you in the morning? Whatever kind of sexual revolution might have taken place over the past thirty years, some unpleasant truths still seemed to apply.

I had no right, he'd said. And, *I can't trust myself...*

He'd been perfectly correct on both points, she acknowledged, wincing. And, almost more tellingly, he had also taught her that she couldn't trust herself.

Fleetingly it occurred to her that it would be terribly simple to blow his ship of happiness right out of the water, but that idea was quashed as soon as it was formed. That was the kind of plan that would appeal to her father, and she was following in his footsteps no longer.

Besides, however wretched she was feeling, she loved Jake, and, God help her, she always would, and nothing—*nothing*—would ever drive her to ruin his life.

When she was feeling more composed, she changed into her simple black *maillot*, donned a wrap and a pair

of espadrilles and went down to the pool. She had it to
herself this afternoon. Gordon was in Nice, and Susan
was planning to wrestle in solitude with the notes for
her book.

Under the shade of an umbrella, Zanna concentrated
on the novel she was reading—a bitter-sweet story of
love and loss that she could well have done without.
When she could bear no more, she put it down and slid
into the sparkling turquoise water.

In her other existence she'd have pounded up and
down, completing length after length as if engaged in
some personal marathon. Now she took things more cautiously, relishing the exercise and sense of well-being
without pushing herself to the limit.

The last stretch she swam underwater, coming up
breathlessly, blindly, into the dazzle of the sunlight as
she reached for the rail.

And felt her wrists firmly clasped, herself drawn forwards and upwards to the steps out of the pool.

She shook her drenched hair out of her eyes, blinking
away the drops of water on her lashes.

He said, 'Good afternoon.' In his light-coloured trousers and dark blue shirt he looked cool and relaxed, but
the dark eyes were watchful, even wary, as they surveyed her.

Nor did it take long to suss out the reason for his
uneasiness. It was standing beside him, its smile revealing the kind of perfect teeth for which American ortho-
dontists were famous. The rest of Cindy Wybrandt was
near ideal as well, Zanna's lightning glance absorbed,
from her gleaming nut-brown hair and the honey-tanned
skin shown off by a brief white cut-off top down to her
endless legs revealed by an equally minute skirt.

'And hello to you.' She'd practised her next greeting
to him so often that the words emerged with all the com-

posure she could have wished, in spite of the fact that she was standing there dripping the entire contents of the pool onto the tiled surround. She even managed a smile to match Cindy's.

'How do you do, Miss Wybrandt? I'm Zanna Westcott, and I've heard so much about you.' And all of it in the last few hours, she refrained from adding.

'And Jake's told me about you too.' The voice was low-pitched, with a trace of Southern drawl. The limpid blue eyes fringed by amazing lashes didn't look as if they missed much. 'Apparently you're his long-lost sister.'

So that was how he wanted to play it, Zanna thought with a pang. She gave a slight shrug, smiled again. 'I'll settle for that,' she agreed lightly.

She trod over to her lounger, retrieved her towel and began to blot off the worst of the moisture, using the fabric as a barrier.

'Did you have a good journey?' She couldn't believe how polite and civilised she sounded, when in reality she'd like to claw the pair of them till they bled.

'Oh, amazing.' Cindy gave a gurgle of laughter. 'Jake drove us down here in that wonderful car of his. All that power just waiting to be released—like sharing a cage with a tiger,' she added with a mock shudder. 'It was a real turn-on.'

The car or the driver? Zanna wondered silently, and decided she'd rather not know.

'And we stayed over in this cute little hotel, like an old millhouse, right on the bank of a river,' the other girl went on dreamily. 'They served dinner on the terrace and there were all these little fireflies darting about. It was so-o-o romantic.'

Nor, thought Zanna, aware she was hurting, did she

want to hear any more. She slid damp arms into her wrap and picked up her bag.

'If you'll excuse me, I'll get back to the house. My mother may need me. I'm a working girl, you know.' She was starting to babble.

'A sister with tact. I can see we're going to be friends.' The words were a mite too sugary. Cindy turned to Jake. 'What do you say, honey? Shall we cool off in the pool after that long, hot ride?'

'Fine.' Jake's tone was equable. 'But we'll need to unpack a bit first—get our swimming things.'

'That doesn't usually bother you, baby.' Cindy moved close, began to unbutton his shirt. 'And we'll have the pool to ourselves, after all.'

Zanna, momentarily transfixed, shook herself into activity. If she didn't move soon, the lovely Cindy would have him stripped, she thought frantically.

She threw an inane 'See you later' over her shoulder, and got herself out of there as fast as her flapping espadrilles would let her.

And she heard following her that throaty gurgle of laughter which, she decided savagely, she could soon learn to hate.

She did not feel any more amiably disposed towards the newcomer when she was finally able to escape to her room after dinner that night.

Cindy's creamy drawl had dominated the conversation at table. She'd been charmingly deferential to Susan and Gordon, sweetly polite to Zanna, and all over Jake like a badly fitting suit. Her coral-tipped fingers had flickered with self-conscious grace from his sleeve to his cheek, smoothing his hair, picking non-existent threads from his jacket throughout the meal.

She'd been wearing a shift dress in a stinging shade

of yellow. A wide bracelet made of plaited white and yellow gold had been clasped round one wrist, with a matching necklet adorning her throat.

They were a gift, she'd told them all coyly, from her daddy, who'd had them made specially for her birthday after he'd vainly trawled the jewellery stores of three states looking for a suitable present.

A wistful glance at her bare left hand had indicated the piece of jewellery she anticipated next.

Zanna had had to stop herself grinding her teeth.

In the *salon* it had been even worse. Cindy had gone overboard for Gordon's hi-fi unit, and had scoured through the CDs, most of which seemed to have some deep, personal meaning for Jake and herself. She'd even insisted they dance together, and Jake hadn't seemed reluctant.

But then, Zanna thought bitterly, as she recalled the circumstances of their own meeting, he liked dancing.

When she'd finished her coffee, she'd made an unobtrusive exit.

She sat for a long time by the window, staring out into the darkness. No moon tonight, but the sky was awash with stars, looking indeed close enough to touch, demonstrating just how and why Les Étoiles had got its name.

In all the vastness of the universe, the problems of one girl on one small planet had to seem ludicrously unimportant. But the pain was there, nevertheless, and it wouldn't go away. Somewhere in the garden an owl hooted, and it was somehow the loneliest sound in the world.

Zanna shivered. It was time she went to bed and tried to forget her troubles in sleep, she thought, getting to her feet. And then she paused, halfway across the room, as someone tapped quietly at her door.

'Who's there?'

'It's Jake.' He rattled the knob impatiently. 'Open the door, Zanna. I need to speak to you. I have something of yours,' he added, when the lengthening pause made it clear she wasn't going to respond.

'Can't it wait until the morning?'

'It nearly is morning,' he reminded her drily. 'And you're not asleep, so what's the problem?'

Reluctantly Zanna crossed to the doorway, switched on the main light, turned the key and threw open her door.

'The problem is,' she said grittily, 'that I didn't want to be disturbed.'

'Then I apologise for my intrusion.' He didn't sound in the least repentant. 'But I thought you'd want to have this.'

'My photo album.' She almost snatched it from him. 'So you took it.'

'I found it on the sofa and borrowed it,' he corrected her. 'So that Susan would know that it wasn't a false alarm. That you'd finally come looking for her.' He paused. 'I should have returned it before, I know, but I've had a lot on my mind.'

She said curtly, 'I can imagine. Well—thanks—I suppose.'

His sudden grin tore at her heart. 'Don't overwhelm me. I thought you'd need it when you set out on your travels.'

'Travels?' she echoed stupidly.

'To the land of Oz. Or have you changed your mind about that?'

'No,' she said quietly. 'No, nothing's changed.' She forced a smile of her own. 'Thank you again, really. And goodnight.' She went to close the door, but he didn't move.

'What have you been doing up here all by yourself?'

She bit her lip. 'Looking at the night sky. It—it's so different here—so much clearer than in London.'

'Or any other city. Blame streetlights and pollution.'

'Yes, of course,' she said with false brightness. 'But stargazing's over for tonight, and I'd really like to get some sleep.'

'I'd say you need it,' he said abruptly. 'You've been looking weary to death all day.'

She wanted to say, Well, hush my mouth. I thought you only had eyes for your Southern belle. But common sense kept her silent. She couldn't let him know that Cindy Wybrandt mattered.

He put out a hand and cupped her chin, tilting it upwards so that he could look into her eyes. 'What is it, Susie?' His voice was very gentle. 'What's wrong?'

Sudden rage possessed her. Oh, God, how dared he? she exploded inwardly. How dared he look at her— speak to her like that, when any moment he was going to walk away from her to the arms of his little Georgia peach, or whatever species of fruit or vegetable she was?

She jerked her chin free. 'I'm perfectly fine, thank you. I simply find the heat here—tiring.'

Jake stepped back. He said courteously, 'Then I won't keep you any longer.'

She watched him walk away, then she closed the door and leaned back against its heavy panels, her eyes tightly closed against the tears which threatened her.

She said aloud, 'How long can I stand this? How much longer…?'

And she could find no answer in her heart.

CHAPTER THIRTEEN

SHE awoke the next morning with a headache.

As she dressed she noticed the sky wasn't quite so relentlessly blue. There was a haze over the sun and a general heaviness in the atmosphere, suggesting a storm in the offing.

When she arrived in the dining room, she found Jake with Gordon and Susan. Of Cindy, there was no sign.

'For this relief, much thanks', Zanna quoted inwardly as she poured herself some fruit juice.

She found that the others shared her misgivings about the weather.

'I think I'll stick close to the house today,' Susan said firmly. 'I've some telephoning I want to do for the party, anyway.'

Jake looked at Zanna. 'What are your plans?'

'Oh, I've got plenty to keep me occupied,' she lied. To begin with she had some paracetamol to track down for this headache, she thought ruefully.

'The horses need exercise,' he said. 'I thought you might like to ride Celestine. If we went at once, we could be back before the weather breaks.'

Her heart missed a beat, but she shook her head. 'I haven't ridden for years.'

'It's not something you forget.'

'I'm not so sure.' She smiled, making a joke of it. 'I don't want to attend my own party in plaster.' Nor was she altogether convinced that horse-riding was the kind of activity her obstetrician would recommend, but she kept that to herself.

She turned to her mother. 'Shall I put yesterday's work on disk and print it out so you can look at it?'

Susan's face lit up. 'Oh, darling, what a good idea. I really feel I'm making progress at last, and it's all thanks to you.'

'Let's hear it for Suzannah.' Jake's tone was silky, but his dark eyes were hard and unamused.

Oh, for heaven's sake, she wanted to yell at him. Is this because I won't come riding with you? How many women do you need dangling on your strings?

Instead she stonily tore off a piece of croissant and dunked it in her chocolate.

When Cindy walked in a few minutes later, yawning prettily and apologising for her lateness, Zanna was glad to have a reason to take herself off to the study.

Once there, she was delighted to discover that her mother was right. All the fragments seemed to be coming together into one cohesive whole at last.

She worked until mid-morning, then, feeling suddenly stifled, took a cup of the fresh coffee Madame Cordet had brought her out into the garden. The birds were hushed and there was no movement in the air.

Suddenly, over the hills, she saw lightning run swiftly and crazily, followed almost at once by the low, sullen rumble of thunder. She thought, So here it comes at last, immediately wondering with a sharp pang of anxiety if Jake was back safely from his ride.

And at the same moment she heard him say her name quietly from the French windows behind her.

Irritated at her own weakness, and at the surge of relief from knowing her fears were groundless, she swung round. 'You don't have to check up on me.' Even to her own ears, she sounded pettish. 'I was coming back inside.'

He shook his head. 'It's nothing to do with that.' The

dark eyes held hers, compelling her to listen. 'My father's had a phone call from an associate of ours in London. It's your father. He's been taken to hospital with a heart attack.'

She said stupidly, 'My father? But that can't be right. He's never ill.'

He said gently, 'It's true, Susie, and I'm afraid it's serious. We think you should go to him. Dad's phoning the airport now.'

She had a sudden vision of her father, helpless in a high white bed, attached to tubes and machines. All that strength and power and brutal force shrunk away to nothing.

She said with a gasp, 'Yes—oh, yes.'

And with a blinding flash and a roar the skies above her opened, and the rain descended like a dark, smothering curtain.

Events after that were forever blurred. She seemed to stand still while activity ebbed and flowed around her.

Susan packed for her, putting the barest essentials in a bag. She heard Gordon say the car was waiting and moved obediently towards the door. Madame Cordet surged towards her and embraced her. *'Courage, mon enfant.'* The sign of the cross was traced on her forehead. Then Susan and Gordon were hugging her, telling her to take care, that they'd be waiting for news.

She smiled uncertainly, took another step forward, and saw Jake standing with Cindy. The American girl wasn't smiling. She looked serious—concerned—as she gazed up at Jake. Her lips were moving in some quiet, private message, then she reached up and kissed him on the cheek.

It was then that Zanna realised that he was carrying a bag too, and stopped. 'No.' Her voice cracked. 'There's no need. I can manage...'

'Don't be a fool.' He took her arm and marched her out, down to the car, under the shelter of the chauffeur's umbrella. 'Did you think we'd let you go alone?'

He put her into the rear passenger seat and got in beside her. Through the rain, Zanna could just make out the worried faces, the hands waving goodbye. She lifted her own hand, nodded and smiled as the car moved forward.

She remembered little of the ensuing journey. They seemed to whisk through the airport and onto a plane. Once they were airborne, Jake ordered a small brandy and made her drink it. She thought afterwards it might have made her sleep.

Reality returned when their taxi drew up outside the hospital.

'You don't have to come in with me.' She halted in front of the glass door. 'I'll be all right. You should— get back. You have—obligations. It was kind of Cindy to let you bring me this far.'

'We won't talk about that now.' His hand was under her arm again. It occurred to her that without his support she might have fallen to her knees. He added almost harshly, 'And you're not sending me away. Not this time.'

At the desk they learned that Sir Gerald was in a private wing, in Intensive Care. It seemed to be miles away, and the last part of the journey was by lift. As the doors opened Zanna saw a group of people standing, waiting for her.

Jake was still holding her, but Susan and Gordon seemed, somehow, to be beside her too. In her mind she heard Madame Cordet's words: *Courage, mon enfant.*

And she knew, even before the doctor spoke, that she was going to need every scrap of courage—because she had come too late, and the strange, bitter, contradictory man who'd been her father was dead.

She was taken into a room with comfortable chairs and flowers on a low table. They brought her tea and told her how sorry they were. They said it had been a massive heart attack not long after he'd arrived at his office that morning. That he'd recovered consciousness briefly just once.

'He was thinking of you, Miss Westcott.' The sister was being comforting. 'He said "Susie" twice. That is your name, isn't it?'

She said, 'Yes,' and forbore to tell them that her father had never used it, that he had been calling for someone else and that she was glad it was so. Because they would never understand.

The only person who could understand was here beside her, and when they left them alone he held her in his arms and let her weep at last for all the bleak and wasted years.

And for this little while, she thought as she clung to him, she could pretend that he was hers.

The study was dim, the heavy curtains still drawn across the windows as a mark of respect. Zanna pulled them open, the rings rattling along the poles. Even with the sunlight pouring in the room seemed oddly empty, its life-force removed. But then the rest of the house was just the same.

It had been a quiet funeral at the local parish church, just as Zanna had wanted. Later, she understood, there would be a memorial service in London.

The new chairman of Westcott Holdings had come, of course. He'd been Sir Gerald's deputy but she doubted whether he'd ever enjoyed much of his confidence. He had a difficult time ahead of him, she thought. There were already rumours of hostile takeover bids.

Among the crowd from Westcotts she'd thought she'd seen Tessa Lloyd, but when they'd emerged from the church the other woman was nowhere to be seen, so she'd decided she must have been mistaken.

She'd invited the mourners back to the house, of course. There'd been coffee, and alcohol for those who wanted it, and plates of tiny sandwiches and vol au vents, and all the other nibbles that seemed appropriate to the occasion. Gradually they'd shaken hands with her and left, one by one, most of them returning to London.

And now, apart from the housekeeper, Mrs Hanson, who was occupied in the kitchen, she had the house to herself.

At her own suggestion, Jake had not come to the funeral. In fact she'd not seen him for a couple of days, and she thought—no, she corrected herself, she *hoped*— he might have returned to the South of France. Once he'd gone, she could start dealing with the pain.

He had taken her from the hospital that evening to a hotel, where he'd reserved a suite. He'd ordered a meal for them and she'd eaten some of it, then gone to her room. And some time in the night, when she'd been trying to weep quietly, he'd come in and lain on the bed beside her, held her again until she'd cried herself to sleep. And when she'd woken in the morning, he was still there.

And she'd had to remind herself quite forcibly that it was wrong to rely on him too much. Wrong, and dangerous too.

She was thankful that he'd only held her and not tried to comfort her by making love to her, because she'd read somewhere, once, that tears were an aphrodisiac.

She would never forget, she thought, how kind he'd

been, and how strong. He'd been there for her all
through the inevitable formalities, although he'd never
touched her again.

He'd been beside her while she spoke to lawyers,
members of the Westcott board and accountants, and
also her father's own doctor, who told her that he'd advised major surgery two years before.

She'd said numbly, 'I never knew.'

'He wouldn't let anyone know,' he'd returned grimly.
'He regarded the whole thing as a sign of weakness and
dismissed it.'

She wished she could do the same with her feelings
for Jake. They'd continued to share the suite at the hotel,
and it had been torture to lie in the darkness each night,
knowing how near he was, yearning for him with every
fibre of her being.

But the crunch had come when she'd entered the sitting room to find him engaged in a low-voiced telephone
conversation. As soon as he saw her standing in the
doorway, he'd swiftly excused himself and replaced the
receiver.

The realisation had come to her that he'd been talking
to Cindy, reminding her cruelly but succinctly that he
had a life of his own elsewhere. A life in which she
could have no part.

Over dinner that night she'd told him quietly and
calmly that she was grateful for all he'd done but that
she was able to cope alone from now on. That she would
be moving out of the hotel and using her father's London
flat as a temporary base.

He'd been silent for a while, then he'd said slowly,
'Yes, that would probably be best.' And there it had been
left.

She'd been surprised to find that Sir Gerald had not

altered his will. She had inherited everything—from his Westcott shareholding down to his racehorses.

Plus, of course, this big, echoing barn of a house—where she'd grown up, where her father had lived his lie and made her an unwitting part of it.

She'd been obliged to come back to it for the funeral, and to sort out whatever personal papers there might be, but she didn't want to spend the night here. She'd already instructed an estate agent to put it on the market, and would be sending the furniture to a saleroom. Everything, that was, except her mother's portrait.

Even now, knowing her mother was alive and well, Zanna found it disturbing. She stared up at it, wondering how her father could have borne to keep it here in this room where he'd spent so much of his time. Or if, in fact, it had been a kind of atonement.

She'd said to Jake, 'Will you tell my mother that he called her name?'

'No,' he'd said. 'No, I don't think so. Unless you particularly wish it?'

She'd shaken her head. 'It's been too long a silence. She'll be happier—not knowing.'

And she wouldn't want the portrait either, Zanna decided. That unhappy faceless woman didn't exist any more. The thing would be better destroyed.

She would go back to London this evening, she thought. She'd arrange to sell the flat as well, as soon as possible, and rent somewhere while she decided what she was going to do with her life. She was still determined to disappear, but the choice of hiding place had opened up considerably.

Her legs were aching, so she went over to the massive desk and sat down behind it. She pulled open the top drawer, but it contained nothing but headed writing paper and envelopes. The other drawers were completely empty—like the house, and the life he'd made for himself, she thought. If there had been some other dimension to his existence, he'd left no clues behind.

She was aware of another presence in the room and thought it was Mrs Hanson, bringing her the bowl of soup and platter of more substantial sandwiches that she'd promised.

She glanced up and found Tessa Lloyd glaring at her from the doorway. She was dressed totally in black and her usually immaculate hair was dishevelled. She looked strange—almost wild, Zanna thought, startled.

She forced a smile. 'Hello, Tessa. I thought I spotted you earlier. Did you miss your lift with the others?'

The other woman didn't reply. She walked forward until she was standing on the other side of the desk. In direct confrontation, Zanna realised, with sudden disquiet. She pushed back her chair and got to her feet, so at least they were on a level.

She said briskly, 'I don't know how you got in, but as you're here may I offer you something—coffee—a drink?'

Tessa Lloyd laughed. 'The perfect hostess. The perfect daughter. What a joke. What a bloody joke.'

She put clenched fists on the desk and leaned forward. She said thickly, 'How dare you sit there, where he did? How dare you take his place, you slut?'

Zanna's heart sank. She thought, I really don't need this.

She drew a deep breath. 'I appreciate you're upset, but this is hardly the time or the place...'

'No?' The other woman shook her head. 'Do you know how it made me feel, seeing you in church today? Playing the chief mourner, you hypocritical bitch.'

'I was his only child,' Zanna said levelly.

'And his heiress too. Let's not forget that.' Tessa gave

a strident laugh. 'All those fools fawning round you, pretending they didn't know he threw you out. That he was planning to cut you off completely—if he'd lived.' Her face worked, and she pressed one hand convulsively to her mouth.

'You killed him,' she went on, her voice rising. 'You know that, don't you, you little slut?'

'Heart disease killed him,' Zanna said flatly. 'He should have had treatment two years ago, and refused. And he could have changed his will. I wouldn't have cared.'

It was true, she thought. She would have swapped Sir Gerald's entire estate for one sign of genuine love and understanding while he was alive. Or for him to have told her the truth. But she wasn't going to say that to Tessa Lloyd.

'That's easily said when here you are, mistress of all you survey,' Tessa sneered. 'He loved this house. After the company, it was the centre of his world. Thank God he can't know that you're living in it now.'

'That's enough,' Zanna said sharply. 'You'd better go.'

'When I'm ready.' There were flecks of spittle on the other woman's lips, and Zanna closed her eyes in revulsion. The other woman must be ill, she thought desperately, nearing a breakdown of some kind. But what could she do? Even with her hands over her ears she couldn't shut out Tessa Lloyd's voice, with its anger and hate.

'It was bad enough he had to endure knowing that you were nothing but a tart—a little whore. At least he's been spared the desecration of seeing your filthy bastard grow up here.'

She gasped suddenly, and was silent.

Zanna, cringing mentally from the onslaught, heard in

total astonishment a familiar voice say quietly and grimly, 'I'd say that's more than enough. Will you leave of your own accord, or do I have to get the police?'

Zanna's eyes flew open. Jake was standing beside Tessa Lloyd, his hand gripping her arm. His dark eyes were blazing from his pale, set face. The other woman recoiled visibly.

'Who the hell are you?' she demanded hoarsely.

'I'm Miss Westcott's future husband,' Jake said. 'And the father of the bastard you spoke of so eloquently.'

Zanna's legs were suddenly shaking under her. She reached behind her for the chair and lowered herself into it.

He went on, too evenly, 'I presume you came in your own car? I suggest you leave by the same means.'

Tessa Lloyd stared up at him. The angry flush had died from her face, and with it the malign energy which had possessed her. Now she seemed crumpled. A shadow of herself.

'You don't understand,' she said tonelessly. 'I—I loved him.'

'I understand love,' Jake said curtly. 'But not the kind of twisted emotion you and your late employer indulged in.' Without relinquishing his grip on her arm, he took her to the door.

'Mrs Hanson?' he called, and said when the house-keeper appeared enquiringly, 'This visitor is leaving now. Perhaps you'd see her to her car and on her way.' He waited until the two women had disappeared from view, then came back into the study, closing the door behind him.

He looked frowningly at Zanna. 'Are you all right?'

'Yes.' She was shaking inside, her heart thudding un-evenly. 'At least—I think so. I—I didn't expect that. I mean—I knew she'd never liked me particularly...'

'I would say that was an understatement,' he said drily.

'Well—thank you for helping.' God, that sounded inane. 'But what are you doing here?'

'I arrived during the funeral,' he said. 'I told Mrs Hanson I needed to talk to you alone, and she kindly let me wait in the kitchen.'

'Oh,' she said, and swallowed. 'I—I thought you'd be on your way back to France.' Back, she thought, to Cindy.

'I'm sure you did,' he said harshly. 'Tell me something, Suzannah. Did you ever intend to break the news to me that you were expecting our child?'

Zanna lifted her chin. 'How do you know it's yours?'

'Because I've had you in my bed,' he said. 'And I know you bear no resemblance to the whore, slut or tart that your recent visitor so picturesquely described. You were sweet, giving, and incredibly innocent. Nothing will ever convince me the baby you're having isn't ours. So, stop playing games and tell me why you said nothing.'

'Because it was too sudden.' Her voice shook. 'It didn't mean anything. It couldn't. It was a one-night stand. The sort of casual sex you're not supposed to have any more. A mistake, as you told me yourself.'

'Yes,' Jake said slowly. 'It was a mistake, quite clearly, because my hunger for you—my greed—totally misled you about my ultimate intentions. I shouldn't have swept you off your feet and into bed like that. I should have kept my head and to some extent my distance—courted you properly.'

He shook his head. 'But I felt as if I was in a dream. I was terrified that I'd wake and find you weren't real. I felt I had to make you mine, to take you and put my mark on you in some totally primitive way.'

He paused, then, 'I'm not proud of it, and when you left as you did I regretted very bitterly that I hadn't been more patient—more in control. Maybe if we had that night over again I'd do things differently. I—I don't know.'

He flung back his head, his face strained. 'As for it being just casual sex—my God, darling, people can live together for twenty years without ever experiencing the kind of physical and emotional harmony, the completeness we had that night. Every time we kissed or touched we were telling each other it was love, it was real and it would be for ever. I thought you knew that as well as I did. That's why I was so shattered when I woke and you were gone. Why I moved heaven and earth to find you.

'Only I was determined that when we did meet again I'd play it cool. Go back to square one and woo you correctly. I told myself that bringing you and Susan together would be a perfect beginning.' Jake shook his head ruefully. 'But when we did meet up, I was the one being kept at a distance. You'd built this fence around you which said "Intruders—Keep Out" and I didn't know what to do—how to get near you. You blocked me at every turn.'

Zanna bent her head. 'I thought you just wanted a physical relationship. I knew I couldn't cope with that.'

'God, I've been so stupid.' His voice was bleak with self-accusation. 'I should have guessed about the baby that day in the gallery, when you fainted at my feet. I suppose I was just too glad to see you to think straight. And, frankly, it was one consequence of that night I hadn't even considered.'

He groaned softly. 'My real nightmare was that either I'd made you hate me or, even worse, that I'd totally misread the situation and you were completely indifferent to me—that all the love, the caring was on my side alone.'

'No,' she said huskily. 'It was never like that. I was in love too, but it just took me longer to recognise the fact. And I did want to tell you about the baby. When I found out I was pregnant, I drove straight to Emplesham to find you.'

Jake groaned again. 'And I wasn't there.'

'And when I did see you everything had changed,' Zanna continued. 'I—I'd had time to think, by then, and I was frightened—scared that you wouldn't want to know, or that you'd try to buy me off.'

She took a deep breath. 'Or even that you'd come up with my father's solution and try to make me have an abortion.'

Jake was very still. 'Is that what he did?' he asked hoarsely. 'Dear God, was that what you fought him about—why you left the company?'

'Yes.' Zanna sighed. 'History repeating itself. Although I didn't know that at the time.'

Jake said something softly and violently under his breath.

'I'm damned if I'm staying on the other side of this desk a moment longer,' he announced, striding round to her side and pulling her to her feet. 'I'm here to ask you to marry me, not be interviewed for a job.'

'You want to marry me?' Her voice was uncertain as he led her to the window-seat. 'But you can't.'

'I think I must.' He was holding both her hands in his. 'Dad and Susan have forbidden me to return without you.'

She bit her lip. 'I don't think they'll be very happy to find out I'm pregnant.'

'I think they'll be ecstatic. Susan will just turn the party she was planning into a wedding reception.'

'But there's Cindy.'

'Indeed there is,' he agreed. 'She's hoping to be chief bridesmaid.'

'Bridesmaid?' She didn't know whether to laugh or cry. 'Oh, I don't understand any of this.'

'Cindy was camouflage,' he admitted, his mouth twisting wryly. 'She's an old friend, and when I had dinner with her and her fiancé a while back they soon realised I was having problems. They wormed it all out of me, told me I'd been an idiot, then suggested that a dose of old-fashioned jealousy might gauge your real feelings.'

Her lips parted helplessly. 'You mean—it was all an act? Oh, I don't believe it.'

'No half-measures with Cindy,' Jake retorted. 'She even surprised me. But she told me she was sure you loved me, only you were fighting it, just like your mother before you, and that I must hang in there and be patient.'

The strong hands holding hers were trembling. 'Was she right, Susie? Will you be my wife—my love—for the rest of our lives?'

She said, 'I will,' and knew that no ceremony would ever make them more husband and wife than at that moment.

She went into his arms, responding freely and joyously to the warm tenderness of his mouth on hers.

It was a long time before he let her go, his arms reluctant as he released her, his eyes smiling into hers.

'Let's go home, Susie,' he said softly. 'All three of us.'

She took his hand and drew it, calmly and trustingly, to the new, gentle rounding of her body.

'Yes,' she said. 'Oh, yes, please, my love.'

MILLS & BOON®

Next Month's Romances

♡

Each month you can choose from a wide variety of romance novels from Mills & Boon. Below are the new titles to look out for next month from the Presents™ and Enchanted™ series.

Presents™

THE PERFECT SEDUCTION	Penny Jordan
A NANNY NAMED NICK	Miranda Lee
INDISCRETIONS	Robyn Donald
SCANDALOUS BRIDE	Diana Hamilton
SATISFACTION GUARANTEED	Helen Brooks
FLETCHER'S BABY!	Anne McAllister
THE VENGEFUL GROOM	Sara Wood
WILLING TO WED	Cathy Williams

Enchanted™

LOVE CAN WAIT	Betty Neels
THE YOUNGEST SISTER	Anne Weale
BREAKFAST IN BED	Ruth Jean Dale
THE ONLY SOLUTION	Leigh Michaels
OUTBACK BRIDE	Jessica Hart
RENT-A-COWBOY	Barbara McMahon
TO MARRY A STRANGER	Renee Roszel
HAUNTED SPOUSE	Heather Allison

FREE!

FOUR FREE
specially selected
Presents™ novels
PLUS a FREE Mystery Gift
when you return this page...

Return this coupon and we'll send you 4 Mills & Boon® Presents™ novels and a mystery gift absolutely FREE! We'll even pay the postage and packing for you.

We're making you this offer to introduce you to the benefits of the Reader Service™– FREE home delivery of brand-new Mills & Boon Presents novels, at least a month before they are available in the shops, FREE gifts and a monthly Newsletter packed with information, competitions, author profiles and lots more...

Accepting these FREE books and gift places you under no obligation to buy, you may cancel at any time, even after receiving just your free shipment. Simply complete the coupon below and send it to:

MILLS & BOON READER SERVICE, FREEPOST, CROYDON, SURREY, CR9 3WZ.

READERS IN EIRE PLEASE SEND COUPON TO PO BOX 4546, DUBLIN 24

NO STAMP NEEDED

Yes, please send me 4 free Presents novels and a mystery gift. I understand that unless you hear from me, I will receive 6 superb new titles every month for just £2.20* each, postage and packing free. I am under no obligation to purchase any books and I may cancel or suspend my subscription at any time, but the free books and gift will be mine to keep in any case.

(I am over 18 years of age)

P7YE

Ms/Mrs/Miss/Mr_____
BLOCK CAPS PLEASE

Address_____

_____

_____ Postcode _____

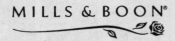

Back by Popular Demand

Anne Mather

COLLECTOR'S EDITION

A collector's edition of favourite titles from one of Mills & Boon's best-loved romance authors.

Don't miss this wonderful collection of sought-after titles, now reissued in beautifully matching volumes and presented as one cherished collection.

Look out next month for:

| Title #3 | **Charade in Winter** |
| Title #4 | **A Fever in the Blood** |

Available wherever Mills & Boon books are sold

DEBBIE MACOMBER

THIS MATTER OF MARRIAGE

Hallie McCarthy gives herself a year to find
Mr Right. Meanwhile, her handsome neighbour
is busy trying to win his ex-wife back. As the two
compare notes on their disastrous campaigns, each
finds the perfect partner lives right next door!

*"In the vein of When Harry Met Sally,
Ms Macomber will delight."*

—Romantic Times

**AVAILABLE IN PAPERBACK
FROM SEPTEMBER 1997**

Meet
A PERFECT FAMILY

Shocking revelations and heartache lie just beneath the surface of their charmed lives.

The Crightons are a family in conflict. Long-held resentments and jealousies are reawakened when three generations gather for a special celebration.

One revelation leads to another - a secret war-time liaison, a carefully concealed embezzlement scam, the illicit seduction of another's wife. The façade begins to crack, revealing a family far from perfect, underneath.

"Women everywhere will find pieces of themselves in Jordan's characters"
–Publishers Weekly

The coupon is valid only in the UK and Eire against purchases made in retail outlets and not in conjunction with any Reader Service or other offer.

- -